Brooke

Brooke and Peter

Cathedral Hills, Volume 3

Morris Fenris

Published by Changing Culture Publications (CCPUB), 2021.

This is a work of fiction. Similarities to real people, places, or events are entirely coincidental.

BROOKE AND PETER

First edition. October 26, 2021.

Copyright © 2021 Morris Fenris.

Written by Morris Fenris.

Morris Fenris

Brooke and Peter

Cathedral Hills Series Book 3

Copyright 2015 Morris Fenris

Changing Culture Publications

All rights reserved. No part of this book may be reproduced or transmitted in any form or by any means, electronic or mechanical, including photocopying, recording or by any information storage and retrieval system without written permission from the author.

Chapter 1

New York City, two weeks earlier...

Brooke Jameson hung up the phone, dropped her head into her hands, and gave way to the tears she'd been holding back. Zachary had left over an hour earlier, and he had forgotten to unplug the phone and take it with him. It was the first time in weeks that had happened, and she'd known this might be her only chance at letting someone know she needed help.

She'd thought about calling the authorities, but Zachary worked for the District Attorney's office, and she knew he was considered the up-and-coming golden boy. *Who would believe her story? She couldn't even believe it and she was living it!* To make matters worse, she knew she'd done this to herself. Oh, maybe not her current predicament, but her actions in the previous months and years had made her current situation possible.

Brooke had come to New York two years ago, thinking she'd finally caught her big break. She'd gone to an open audition while still in high school, and a few weeks later had received a modeling contract and plane tickets to California. She had gotten on the plane a little over six years ago, just out of high school, with stars in her eyes and a smile on her beautiful face. Those first four years her life had been fast paced, and so different from Cathedral Hills that she had readily embraced all it had to offer. The good and the bad.

As her modeling career had taken off, she'd found herself having more and more trouble relaxing and getting enough sleep. Her schedule had been crazy, and the more successful she became, the worse it got. When her manager had suggested that she see his physician, she'd agreed. The doctor had prescribed her a low dose sleeping pill, which she had reluctantly agreed to take. Months later, she was unable to sleep without their aid.

And then two years ago, it looked like things had changed for the better. Her California agent had introduced her to an agent who worked exclusively with magazines published in South America. The pay was fantastic, and she'd been assured that this was the next step in cementing her worldwide modeling career. She'd flown to New York City for a photo shoot, and left feeling extremely optimistic about her chances of being chosen. The fact that the garments she'd been asked to wear were more revealing than she usually was comfortable with was swept aside by the promise of fame and fortune.

When she'd landed an exclusive modeling contract with that same agency a few weeks later, she'd wasted no time in closing up shop in California and moving to New York City. She had been so excited! The job had included travel to all sorts of exotic places, and she had been so caught up in the adoration she'd been receiving, she hadn't realized the peril she'd been in.

Her California agent had been instrumental in helping her secure the job, and when he'd suggested that she continue taking the sleeping pills through the transition, she'd readily agreed. She hadn't wanted to do anything that might jeopardize her ability to meet the terms of her contract.

The stress of traveling had been overwhelming, and a few weeks into her first trip abroad, she'd been given what she thought were muscle relaxers by one of the photography assistants. They seemed to have worked, and life went on. She modeled very risqué evening gowns while draped over expensive sports cars, and became a much sought-after arm ornament for the rich playboys of the world. Her agent took care of all the details, and she simply went along with everything while her bank balance continued to grow.

Slowly, the outfits she'd been asked to model had become more risqué, and soon she was modeling swimsuits and lingerie exclusively. She rarely saw the finished photos, trusting her New York agent when he told her they were fabulous. That had been a major mistake.

A little over a year into her new contract, she had been contacted about her mother's Alzheimer's. She'd been planning a trip home to see what help she might offer, and she knew that her parents would be interested in seeing some of her recent photos. She'd gone by the agent's office, intending to ask for copies of some of the tamer photos, but he hadn't been there. While looking through a pile of papers lying on his desk, she had stumbled across one of the magazines laying on her agent's desk.

That had been five months earlier, and she was still embarrassed and appalled at what she'd seen that day. She'd ignored her facial expressions, focusing instead on the bare skin that was so alluringly revealed. She was kneeling in the sand with the ocean waves behind her, and she hadn't realized that the swimsuit left almost nothing to the imagination. The photographer had done an excellent job of making her look like one of the swimsuit models that graces the more popular sports magazines each year. Unfortunately, the pictures made her feel dirty and embarrassed.

She'd rifled through his desk some more and found other such magazines, all of which she played an integral part in. When she stumbled across a small flyer with her picture on it, she almost fainted. The writing was in Spanish, but she was able to pick out enough to realize the paper was an advertisement for her escort services. She found more pictures of herself in skimpy outfits, and she knew she should have paid closer attention to what was going on with her career. *Her agent had turned her from a model into a highly paid escort!*

She'd waited for her agent, Marco Pellinni, to show up, and then accused him of tricking her into modeling for a porn magazine and turning her into an escort. The other photos in the magazines had been of the same caliber, with many of them showing girls completely undressed, with only the bare essentials covered. And nowhere had she seen anything actually selling the swimsuit, or other clothing items she was wearing. Instead, there had been multiple ads for call girls and mail-order brides. Even a few 1-900 numbers advertising beautiful women waiting to talk to you for only a few dollars a minute.

She'd waved the escort flyer in front of his face and demanded to know if all of her recent high-profile dates had merely been business transactions. Marco hadn't even had the good grace to deny her accusations or defend himself. He'd simply told her she needed to calm down. She'd been paid very well for being seen with those men, and she needed to look at the bigger picture.

Brooke had been furious about being used in such a way and refused to do any more photo shoots for him, or the magazine. She also refused to go on any more high-profile dates. When Marco had threatened her, she'd flown home a few days earlier than planned. Memories of that visit filled her with guilt, as she remembered having been emotionally distant from everyone, even her ailing mother.

Unfortunately, distance hadn't stopped Marco's attempts to get her back in the fold. He'd repeatedly called her cell phone, at all times of the day and night. When she returned to New York, she'd immediately changed her number. When he began having men come to her apartment at all hours of the night, threatening her if she didn't honor the contract, she went to the District Attorney's office to file a complaint. Her thought had been that whatever was going on was more than likely illegal, and since her picture was all over the magazines and escort flyers, she wanted legal protection when the authorities finally acted. It had only taken her a few days after returning to New York City to reach that point. Marco was destroying her sanity, and she admitted to herself that she was actually afraid for her life!

She'd met Zachary Grayson there, and he'd simply swept her off her feet. He'd promised her the full protection of the law and had even offered to speak with Marco directly. Almost immediately, the threatening phone calls and nightly visits had ceased. Brooke had been so relieved, she'd not even questioned what kind of legal action was being taken against Marco and his other business associates. Lack of sleep, and days of fear and worry, had taken their toll on her, emotionally and physically.

Zachary had told her very little after questioning her that first day, and since she'd never been involved in any sort of legal action before, she didn't question anything he told her. The only piece of information she'd ferreted out was that Marco and her agent in California had been working together.

Zachary had been her knight in shining armor. He'd been attentive, always complimenting her; and three weeks later, when he'd asked her to move in with him, she had done so without a second thought. Zachary had taken over her life, and she hadn't even put up a token protest. He'd seemed so attentive and caring, keeping her from unwanted media attention, protecting her privacy, and even having his own physician and trainer come to the penthouse so she didn't have to worry about being seen in the city.

She'd been very fearful in the first few weeks after seeing those magazines, but Zachary had assured her they were only published and distributed in South America; so she had no worries about someone in the city recognizing her. She hadn't realized that Zachary was part of the problem, and several weeks later, she had signed her name to the bottom of a marriage license in a judge's office.

She rubbed her temple, the ache becoming more pronounced with her tears. She hadn't realized anything was truly wrong until a few weeks ago, when Zachary had gone out of town unexpectedly. He'd never wanted her to work after they got married, telling her that he preferred that she keep a low profile until the court case against her former agents was finished up. When she'd asked about the time frame for that to occur, Zachary had been less than encouraging, saying that similar cases had taken years to come to judgment.

Brooke had been relieved, and initially enjoyed the small vacation, but soon she found herself becoming bored and restless. Zachary had demanded that she speak with a counselor, who had prescribed her some anxiety pills to help her as she dealt with the aftermath of having been used so callously for profit.

As days, and then weeks, went by, Brooke found herself becoming more and more afraid to leave the apartment without Zachary by her side. She'd started having nightmares, for which yet more pills had been prescribed. It seemed to be a vicious cycle, and Zachary easily took over running her life.

She was still in high demand as a model, but Zachary had taken over the role of her agent, as well, and she only did exclusive photo shoots now. Zachary took care of everything from the shopping, to arranging for beauticians to visit the apartment so she didn't have to sully her feet on the streets of New York City, to managing her financial portfolio for her.

She had placed all of her furniture, unneeded belongings, and her newly purchased Mustang in storage the week she'd moved in with him, not knowing how long those living arrangements would last. By the time she'd said "I do," she'd all but forgotten her former life, and Zachary seemed content to leave it forgotten. She'd paid the storage fees a year ahead, not wanting to mess with a monthly payment, and in her altered mental state, had all but erased her former possessions from her mind.

Slowly, he'd encouraged her to stop communicating with those back home who cared for her. *You don't want them to know what you got mixed up in, do you? What would your parents or brother say if they ever saw those photographs? It's better to just distance yourself until everything is settled in the courts. I'm not sure how much longer I can keep the pictures in evidence from the media.*

Brooke had let her guilt escalate, until she was happy to stay in the penthouse and do nothing but watch television most of the day. Zachary had installed some exercise equipment in a spare room for her use, and had even gotten her some special vitamins to help keep her in tip-top shape.

Everything had seemed to be going fine, until Zachary had gone out of town unexpectedly. He hadn't known that she was out of her special vitamins, and she'd chosen not to say anything to him, because she didn't want to inconvenience him. She'd foolishly thought they were only vitamins, and once he returned to town, he could get them replaced for her.

She'd been so wrong! Over the next two days, she'd experienced stomach cramps, massive headaches, chills, and hallucinations, that eventually had her attempting to reach someone outside the apartment. Her skin had felt like it was covered with insects, and she'd been unable to put a coherent thought together. She was sure she'd been poisoned by something she ate, and after suffering for more than a day, she knew she needed to find some help.

It hadn't occurred to her until that day that there were no phones in the apartment. Zachary almost always used a cell phone, and the landline phone he used was a special coded phone he used for business matters. He'd explained to her that it had some special software installed that prevented the calls from being traced, and in his line of work for the DA's office, he often used the phone, even in his downtown office.

Whenever he plugged it in at home, he always made sure to unplug it, and tuck it away inside his briefcase when he left for the day. Her cell phone and laptop computer were somewhere in the apartment, since she'd arrived with them, but she hadn't seen them in weeks. *Or was it months?* She'd lost all track of time; and though she made a cursory look through the apartment, they were nowhere to be found.

Thinking to seek help from the porter at the front entrance to the apartment building, she'd found enough strength to dress herself, but when she'd tried to open the door to the penthouse, she'd found it locked. From the outside. She'd become even more frightened when she realized she was stuck in the apartment until Zachary saw fit to come home. She'd panicked, falling headlong into a panic attack of major proportions.

Zachary had come home the next day to find her sick, irrational, and irate. She'd demanded he take her to a hotel, throwing whatever was in reach at him, but her weakened state only allowed her a few moments to rage at him before her strength gave out. She'd collapsed on the floor of the apartment, her stomach heaving, as chills raced up and down her spine. Things might have gone better if he'd apologized, or at least seemed somewhat upset at having trapped her inside their apartment, but that hadn't been his reaction.

Zachary's response had been to call a family friend, who was a doctor, and have her medicated. She'd overheard him telling the doctor that she had a problem with addiction to prescription narcotics, and suddenly everything she'd experienced the previous forty-eight hours made sense. She'd been suffering from withdrawals! Zachary had been drugging her, and she'd been helping him.

She'd recovered, with Zachary keeping a close watch on her, and she'd become much more suspicious of his behavior from there on out. She'd tried her best to present the same easy going, complacent personality she knew he'd come to expect, taking special note of everything Zachary gave her. Zachary had been none the wiser, and she had been patiently waiting for him to slip up and give her a way out.

She'd even lulled him into a false sense of security by pretending to care less about her friends and family back in Colorado. Since meeting him, Zachary had always insisted she send a basic email to let her family know she was okay, to keep them from worrying.

When she'd announced she no longer felt the need to do that anymore, with hopes that someone would become alarmed and start looking for her, Zachary had told her with a smile that he would be happy to send out a basic email to let everyone know she was doing okay.

Brooke had smiled and continued pretending to be the doped up wife he took out occasionally to show off. She had been secretly planning to escape the next time he took her someplace, but since her incident with the doctor, she hadn't left the apartment once. The toll of pretending nothing had changed was becoming harder to bear, and when she'd awakened to see the phone still plugged in, she'd been ecstatic.

She'd wasted no time in calling her brother's house. She didn't have a clue as to what she was going to say, but surely Tyler would be able to help her. Somebody needed to help her! The call had not gone as planned.

Peter had been at the house. Her heart hurt as she remembered the smiling eyes of the only boy who'd ever owned her heart. He'd been planning to marry her, until she'd been invited to California. He'd stepped aside, allowing her to pursue her dreams, and now she realized she'd thrown away her only chance for true happiness. *God, I've been such a fool! Help me get out of this mess!*

She laughed at herself when she realized the direction her thoughts had gone. It had been a long time since she'd asked God for something, or even just paused to check in with Him. *And you expect Him to help you now? Good luck with that, sweetie.*

She dried her tears, and noticed her hands were shaking badly once again. She'd been slowly weaning herself off the drugs; having tried to do it all at once, and suffering horrible side effects as a result. Not wanting to let Zachary know she was onto his game, she'd been slowly decreasing the dose of her *special vitamins* that she consumed each day.

She reached for the vitamin bottle, and carefully broke one of the tablets in half. She took one half, and then walked to the bathroom and flushed the rest of the tablet down the toilet. *So much for thinking I could go without these stupid pills.*

She returned to the luxuriously decorated living room, and stared out of the large picture windows at the New York skyline. *I wish I was still in Cathedral Hills.* She wrapped her arms around herself, and then headed for the bedroom. With nothing else to do, she would watch television, and hopefully slip into a dreamless sleep, where the nightmare her life had become would fade away for a few short hours. Maybe when she woke she'd try Tyler again, if Zachary hadn't remembered the phone and come home to retrieve it.

Chapter 2

P*resent day...*
Peter exited the New York City airport terminal, and immediately longed for the clean air of the Colorado Mountains. The New York air was heavy with the smell of exhaust, road tar from the recently repaired road in front of him, and a number of other odors he didn't find pleasant at all.

He stepped to the small waiting platform with a taxi sign fixed above it, and then looked at the emailed information Tyler had sent him earlier. According to the marriage license that had been found online, Brooke Jameson had married Zachary Grayson four months ago. There was an address listed, but when Peter had googled it, the address came up as belonging to the New York City District Attorney's office. *A dead end.*

A yellow cab approached, and stopped in front of him. He tucked his suitcase inside and then climbed in. He gave the only address he had to the driver, and then tried to come up with a plan of attack once he got there.

Glancing at his watch, he realized it was already 4 o'clock in the afternoon, and he only hoped there would still be someone in the government office who might know of Zachary Grayson, and where he could be found.

He paid the exorbitant taxi fare when they reached the justice building, and then entered the building and stopped to look at the directory. A security station was set up in the center of the foyer, preventing anyone from entering the rest of the building without going through a metal detector and physical pat down. *Crime must be alive and well in New York.*

He saw that the District Attorney's office occupied both the seventh and the eighth floors. *Well that narrows it down.* Approaching the security guard station, he smiled and waited for one of the uniformed men to acknowledge his presence.

"Can I help you?" the younger of the two men asked, his name tag identifying him as Brad.

"I hope so. I'm looking for Zachary Grayson, and was wondering if one of you could direct me to his office?"

"Do you have an appointment with Mr. Grayson?"

Ah, so this is where he works! Step one accomplished. "Not really. I'm a friend of his wife's. I was in town for just a few hours, and was hoping to take them both to dinner."

"Well, I doubt he's still here this late in the day, but I can call up to his office and check."

"Thanks. That would be very helpful." Peter tucked his hand in his front pocket as he waited.

"Sorry, he's already left for the day. Would you like me to see if he has an emergency number on file? I could give him a call on that."

"No, I have his cell phone number. I'll give it a call." Peter started to move away, and then turned back on an afterthought, "Do you know if they kept their apartment in the city?" He heard that most people who worked in the city kept an apartment there as well, because the traffic was so bad. Hopefully, that was true for the unknown Zachary Grayson. He was fishing for information, and mentally crossed his fingers that he'd catch something besides a dead end.

"Hey, Stan, did Mr. Grayson keep his dad's penthouse apartment after he got married?"

"I believe so. Who wants to know?"

"This guy says he's a friend of Miss Brooke's, and was in town for a few hours. He was wanting to surprise her."

Stan nodded his head, "I'm pretty sure he still has that apartment on the Upper East Side. It's been in the Grayson family for decades. His daddy used it when he was the DA."

"There you go," the uniformed officer named Brad told him with a smile. "Do you remember how to get to the apartment?"

Peter laughed, "Honestly, I'm so turned around once I get down in all these tall buildings – No. Where I come from, you can see for miles, and I navigate by which mountain range is in front of me."

Both security guards laughed, with Stan commenting, "I know how that goes. I grew up in Ohio. We didn't have your mountains, but I never remember getting lost either." The man pulled a sheet of paper towards him and then jotted down an address, "Just give that to the taxi driver and he'll know how to get you there."

"Thanks buddy. That's really nice of you." Peter reached out and shook both uniformed security guards' hands. It never hurt to make friends, and since he had no idea of what he was walking into, having a friend in Zachary's office could come in handy.

"Yeah, don't mention it. And I truly mean that. Don't mention it. To anyone." Brad winked at him, as did Stan.

Peter finished shaking Brad's hand and assured them, "Don't worry, I won't tell a soul about this conversation." He crossed his fingers over his heart, and then held up a two-finger salute, "Scout's honor. You all have a nice evening now." *No need for them to know he'd never been part of a scout troop.*

"You too. I hope Miss Brooke likes her surprise."

"I'm sure she will," he commented, as he turned and walked away. Peter exited the building, dragging his small suitcase behind him, and flagged down another taxi. He handed the piece of paper to the turban-clad man, the smell of curry and some other spice making his eyes water. The sound of Indian music filled the interior of the cab, and Peter decided that New York City was just full of new experiences; many to be had inside a taxi cab.

He sat in the back of the taxi, watching the cars move slowly, like an inchworm along a stick. He glanced out the windows at the other vehicles, and noticed that more than half of the cars on the street were taxis cabs. *Did no one in this town drive themselves?*

Twenty minutes later, the traffic started to thin out, and Peter breathed a sigh of relief. He still hadn't figured out what he was going to say to Brooke when he saw her. *Hey! Remember me? I'm the man you were supposed to marry, instead of some unknown guy your family's never heard of.* He discarded that idea. The old Brooke wouldn't have appreciated his sarcasm. *But then again, the old Brooke would have never dropped off the face of the earth and married some unknown guy. And not told her family or friends about it!*

"Here you are," the driver announced, coming to a stop in front of a lavish apartment building that stood at least twenty floors high.

He paid the taxi fare, grimacing as he realized that he was going to have to find an ATM if he kept going through cash this fast. He pulled his suitcase out of the cab, and then made his way to where a uniformed porter stood on the red carpet leading into the building.

"Good evening, Sir. May I help you find someone?" the older man asked. He was a tall man, only an inch or two shorter than Peter's 6'4", with white hair that was covered by a brimmed hat. His red, double breasted coat stretched over his ample stomach, and Peter immediately wondered if he had ever lost one of the gold buttons from the strain upon the fabric.

"I was looking for the Grayson residence," Peter told him with a smile.

The man looked at his suitcase and then back to his eyes, "Were they expecting you?"

Peter shook his head, "No. I'm in town for a few hours, and I'm a friend of Brooke's."

"Well, I will call up, but Mr. Grayson asked for his car to be brought around in half an hour, as he and Mrs. Grayson were going out for the evening."

"Oh, that's too bad." Peter appeared to be undecided about his next action, and then nodded his head, "Well, I wouldn't want to disrupt their plans. I'll be back in town in a week. I'll give them a call from the airport and make arrangements to meet up with them then." Peter nodded at the man, and then waved for the taxi driver to wait.

"Are you sure you don't want me to call up and let them know you're here?"

"No, really. I'd much rather it be a surprise when I come back. Brooke would feel badly if she knew I was down here and she couldn't spend any time with me."

The porter looked unsure of himself, but then he nodded, "Very good. Have a nice flight to wherever your final destination is this evening."

Peter nodded to the man, "Thanks. I look forward to seeing you again in a week."

"Very good, Sir."

Peter climbed back inside the taxi and then asked his driver, "Feel like playing a little game?"

"A game?" the taxi driver asked.

"Yeah. See, I'm here to see an old friend of mine, but she doesn't know I'm in town. She's getting ready to go out with her husband, and I want to follow her, and then surprise her at dinner."

"You wish to stalk this woman?" the driver asked, with unease in his voice.

"No! No! I don't want to stalk anyone. I just want you to follow her because I'm not sure which restaurant they're headed to. I'll make it worth your while," Peter told him, holding up a hundred dollar bill.

"Oh...I can do that. We will park just inside the garage; that way, they cannot leave without us seeing them do so."

"Brilliant plan."

The driver drove around the block, and then pulled into the small parking garage situated beneath the apartment building, "We will wait here. You tell me when you see their car leave."

Peter nodded his head, and started scanning the parking garage for movement. Ten minutes later, the elevator doors opened, and he watched as an unknown man escorted a very skimpily clad Brooke out and towards a black sports car.

Peter tried not to dwell on what she was, or wasn't, wearing. He kept his eyes trained on her face and was stunned at the blankness of her expression. She almost acted bored!

"You wish me to follow them?" the taxi driver asked.

"Yes, but stay back far enough they can't see us."

"Will do." The taxi set off after the dark black sports car, keeping several vehicles in between them as it slowly made its way back downtown. It finally came to a stop in front of a very exclusive restaurant and nightclub, and Peter cringed as he looked down at what he was wearing.

Worn denim jeans, a button-down blue chambray shirt, with a leather belt and buckle wrapped around his waist. Worn western boots completed his attire – definitely not up to New York standards.

As he sat there, he saw a delivery truck go down the alley behind the building. Several men got out of the vehicle, and began carrying boxes from their delivery van into the back of the restaurant.

Peter leaned forward and gestured towards a side street a block away, "Do me a favor. Pull your cab down there and just park. I'm going to see just how swanky this place is and I'll be right back."

"Why do you not just go in the front door?" the driver asked, confused.

"Did you see what I was wearing when I got in your cab? I'll stick out like a sore thumb, and that would embarrass Brooke; the exact opposite of what I'm here to do."

When the cab driver nodded his head, Peter slid out of the cab and hurried down the alley. He grabbed a stack of boxes, and held them in front of him as he headed towards the propped open door. He passed several men coming out of the restaurant, and one of them told him, "Down the hallway to your left."

"Got it," Peter told the unknown man, and turned towards his left. He could hear soft music coming from his right, and the distinct sounds of a working kitchen to his left. He set his stack of boxes down with the others, and then headed back to the hallway. Instead of exiting, he turned to his left and slid into the back of the nightclub portion of the building.

The dark walls and ceilings, accompanied by dim lighting, aided him in his attempt to remain undetected. He could see groups of people gathered around small tables, or enjoying themselves on the dance floor. What he didn't immediately see was Brooke.

He let his eyes slowly scan the large room, and then he spotted her in the back corner with the man she'd left the apartment with. He assumed the man was her husband, Zachary Grayson.

He watched as they were joined by several other gentlemen, all of whom paid what Peter deemed an inappropriate amount of attention to Brooke. He couldn't see her face clearly, but even from a distance, he could read her body language. She was uncomfortable and barely tolerating the unwanted attention.

When an older man took her arm and pulled her towards the dance floor, Peter couldn't believe she didn't put up a struggle, or object. The man had his hands all over her back, and was holding her much too close. Much too close! Peter was livid on her behalf, and then they turned around so he could see her face. Her eyes were filled with unshed tears, and Peter immediately knew that something was not right with this situation.

When the music stopped, Brooke excused herself and headed towards the opposite side of the dance floor. Peter stayed close to the walls and followed her, relieved to see she was only heading towards the women's washroom.

He waited for a few minutes, but when she didn't come out, he grew concerned that his opportunity to speak with her alone was almost gone. Stepping up to the bathroom door, he gently tapped on the wooden door, and then pushed the door open a crack. "Brooke?" he whispered loudly, lest there be other occupants in the elegantly appointed room.

Hearing no answer to his question, he decided to chance it, and slid through the opening. He pushed the door shut behind him, engaging the deadbolt as he did so. He bent over and was relieved to see only one pair of feet beneath the stalls. "Brooke?"

He heard a sniffle, and then a soft voice, "Tell Zachary I'll be right out."

Tell Zachary? "Brooke? It's Peter."

"Peter?" her voice came again, a little higher pitched and confused. A few seconds later the stall door opened, and she emerged from the stall with a look of shock on her face. "Peter? What are you doing here?"

Peter looked at her and could see that she was almost too thin. Though her makeup was expertly done, her skin had a slight pallor to it, as if she hadn't spent any time in the sun for months. "Are you okay?"

She nodded once, and then asked again, wringing her hands at the same time, "What are you doing here? Does Zachary know you're here?"

Peter shook his head, "No one knows I'm here. After you called home a few weeks ago, everyone realized that something wasn't right, and I came out here to find you. I stopped by your apartment, but you and your husband were headed out."

Brooke looked like she was going to be sick, "You know about my marriage?"

"I don't know that I would go that far. Michelle found a copy of your marriage license on line when she was researching the phone number you called from."

"Michelle?" Brooke's face fell, and the tears that she'd been so valiantly trying to hold back spilled over.

Chapter 3

She felt the tears run over her cheeks and drip onto her chest. "I...Peter..."

Peter couldn't stand to see her so upset, and he slowly approached her, pulling her into his arms when she didn't put up any resistance. It had been years since he'd last held her in his arms, but the old feelings he had for her hadn't faded one bit. *I still love her!*

"Brooke, what's going on here?" He started to run his hands up and down her back, and then realized the entire back of her dress was missing. Instead, he simply wrapped his arms around her and hugged her close for a moment, relishing the way she leaned into him after a few seconds. They stayed that way for several long heartbeats, but then reality returned.

"I've been such a fool," she told him, pushing away from his chest to pace the small distance of the bathroom. "He's going to come looking for me if I don't get back out there soon."

"Who's going to come looking for you? Your husband?"

Brooke nodded nervously, "Yeah. Zachary doesn't like it when I'm out of his sight for very long."

"Sounds like he's a controlling jerk," Peter said before he could stop himself. He started to apologize, but then her murmured words registered.

"You don't know the half of it."

Peter looked at her and then asked her, "Brooke, do you want to stay here? In New York? Is that why you were trying to contact Tyler? Are you in trouble?"

Brooke wrapped her arms around herself as another bout of shivers wracked her body. Zachary hadn't given her any advance notice of tonight's little party, or the fact that she was expected to entertain his guests, and then pose for some photos with them later. The man who'd pulled her to the dance floor was running some sort of political campaign, and seemed to think that having a beautiful woman hanging on his arm would help his chances of winning an election.

Brooke disagreed, but then again, she hadn't been asked for her opinion. Since she hadn't been forewarned, she'd gone all day long without taking anything, and hadn't had a chance to grab even half a pill; not with Zachary watching her every move. As far as he knew, she should have taken her *vitamins* with her lunch, and there should have been plenty of the drug still in her system for tonight's event.

She shivered again, and Peter noticed right away. "Are you cold?"

She shook her head, and then regretted the motion. *Great, now my head is going to get in on the action. If my stomach decides to get involved too, Zachary will know something's not quite right, and my chance of getting away from him...*

She looked up at Peter, and then walked to him, taking his hands in her own as she searched his eyes. "How did you get here?"

"A taxi. I had it follow you from the apartment. He's waiting for me a block away."

Brooke smiled, her heart feeling a glimmer of hope for a brighter future for the first time in weeks. "Let's go." She turned towards the door, pulling him behind her.

"Wait! Where are we going?"

"Away! Please, we have to hurry before he comes looking for me." When Peter didn't seem to share her urgency, she turned to him, "Please! Peter, you're my only hope right now. Please, get me away from here."

Peter didn't understand what was going on, but he could see the fear in her eyes, and hear the desperation in her voice. "Easy, Brooke. If you want to leave the restaurant, I'll take you home. Why don't you go tell..."

She shook her head vehemently, "You don't get it. Zachary can't know where I am, or he'll never let me leave. I know this doesn't make much sense, but I promise to explain everything. Just, make sure the coast is clear, and get me out of the restaurant. Please?"

Peter nodded his head, and then pulled her to stand behind him, "Fine. Let me make sure there's no one out in the hallway." He pulled the door open and then exited the room, feeling her holding onto the back of his shirt as he quickly made his way along the back wall, and back to the hallway next to the kitchen.

He didn't pause, but headed for the back door. Once outside, he reached behind him and pulled her to walk next to him, noticing that she was having trouble keeping up because of the high heels she was wearing. "Those were not meant for walking long distances," he nodded towards her feet.

Brooke looked down and then gave him a hesitant smile, "No, they weren't." She looked back over her shoulder nervously, and then tried to hurry her steps, "Where is this taxi you said was waiting for you?"

"Across the street, just there," he replied, pointing towards the cab that was sitting on the opposite street corner.

Peter stepped onto the sidewalk and waved to get the driver's attention. He was pleased when the man waved back and then pulled out into traffic. "He's going to come to us." He noticed that she kept looking back down the alleyway, and then towards the front of the restaurant, as if she expected someone to come chasing after her. *Oh Brooke, darlin', what did you get yourself mixed up in?*

The taxi driver pulled up, and Peter helped Brooke into the back before sliding in next to her. "Back to her apartment..."

"No! I can't go back there. Don't you have a hotel room or something..."

Peter looked at her attire and then asked, "Don't you want to go home and change clothes?"

"No! Please, I can't go back there." She paused for a moment to marshal her thoughts, and then took a deep breath. She asked the driver if he could take them to a different address. When the driver nodded, she seemed to relax.

"Where did you tell him to take us?"

"Some storage units. My stuff is there, and I can get a change of clothes and pick up my car all at the same time."

"Brooke, what's going on?" Peter asked her, holding her stare with his own brown eyes.

Brooke grew quiet, lost in her own thoughts as she tried to cope with her body's withdrawals from the drugs, and the realization that she needed to get as far away from New York City as possible. Immediately. Do not wait till morning. Do not pass go. Do not collect two hundred dollars. She needed to leave. Now!

"Peter, how long were you planning on staying in the city?" she asked, changing the topic.

"I really didn't have a set plan. I only came out here to see if you were okay. I've already ascertained the answer to that is no, so tell me what I can do to help you."

"I'm leaving."

"What do you mean, leaving?"

"I need to get out of the city. As soon as Zachary realizes I'm not at the restaurant, he'll have every cop in the city looking for me. You don't know him, but he works for the DA's office and has lots of connections. Everyone loves him and won't hesitate to help him, even if it involves skirting the rules."

Peter was quiet for a moment, and then he told her, "I'll make you a deal. You let me tag along with you, wherever you're going, and after we get someplace you deem safe, you tell me everything that's going on here."

Another shiver wracked her body as she nodded, "Fine." She hated that her teeth were chattering, but then her stomach got in on the action, and she swallowed convulsively as the urge to vomit captured her attention.

Peter saw her shiver and then the color drain from her face, "Are you sick?"

Brooke shook her head, "No! Withdrawals." She saw his look of shock, and hurried to assure him, "It's not what you're thinking, and I will explain everything, but right now I need this cab to stop."

Peter told the driver to pull over, and then watched helplessly as Brooke opened her door and emptied her stomach onto the pavement. He took the handful of tissues the driver handed over the backseat, and the bottle of water.

When she was finished and leaned back into the cab, he handed her first the tissues, and then the water. "Do you need a doctor?"

Brooke shook her head, "I'm fine. Or, I will be." She turned to look at him, "In case I forget to say it, thank you for caring enough to come find out what was going on."

"Don't thank me just yet. I still don't know much."

"Thank you, anyway." She was prevented from commenting further, because the taxi arrived at the address she'd given him.

"Do you folks need me to wait around?" the driver asked.

"No," Brooke said with a shake of her head.

"I guess not. Thanks for everything." Peter paid the fare, including the extra hundred dollars he'd promised the man.

"You sure you'll be okay here?" the driver asked, looking around at the deserted location that didn't even have the benefit of street lights. He handed Peter a business card with a phone number on it, "That's my cell phone number. If you need a ride back to town, call me and I'll come back."

Peter thanked the man again, and then took his suitcase and joined Brooke where she stood at the security gate. "Do you have a key to get in here?"

"Don't need one. It's coded with a personal security code I gave them when I put my stuff in here. I was afraid I would lose a key."

"Why do you still have stuff in storage if you've been married for over four months?" Peter wanted to know.

Brooke looked at him, but didn't answer. Instead, she opened the gate, and then waited for him to follow her inside before shutting it with a load bang of metal on metal. She walked through the rows of storage units until she came to the one she wanted. She carefully entered a code into the keypad, and then smiled when a green light blinked. The walk-through door unlocked and she turned the handle, "Wait for just a minute. There's a light inside if I can just find the switch."

Seconds later, the inside of the storage unit lit up, and he was surprised to see a cherry red Mustang sitting in the middle of the unit, surrounded by shelving, boxes, and covered furniture. She lovingly ran a hand over the hood of the car, and felt the same sense of excitement she'd had the first time she'd driven the vehicle.

She'd received a huge bonus from Marco, and purchased the vehicle only days before seeing the magazines lying on his desk. Things had moved so quickly thereafter, she'd taken the easy way out, and stuck everything in storage. Now, she was taking the first step towards reclaiming her life.

"Wow! That's some car," Peter whistled, walking around the Mustang, and admiring the black leather interior and soft top.

"Thanks," she told him, although she'd already decided that once she was someplace safe, the car would have to go. Knowing where the bonus money had come from, she didn't think she could stomach owning the car for very long. Right now, it was simply a means to an end.

"Let me grab some clothes, and we'll be ready to go."

"Where exactly are we headed?" Peter asked, watching as she rummaged through a few boxes and began pulling out clothing and shoes.

Brooke shook her head, "I really don't know. Someplace away from New York. Actually, probably away from the East Coast. Zachary seems to know everyone, and I need someplace to think and figure out what my next move is."

"Can I ask you a question?" Peter asked.

"Sure. I don't know if I'll answer it, but you can ask."

"Why did you marry him?" Peter queried, really wanting to know what had possessed her to do something so out of character.

Brooke looked at him and then sighed, "Honestly, I don't know that I truly had any say or choice in the matter." She grabbed a pair of jeans, a t-shirt, and a few other articles of clothing before ducking behind a stack of tall boxes. "I do know that I don't want to be married to him any longer."

"That doesn't make any sense. You've only been married for four months, according to the paperwork Michelle found."

"I know," she said, her voice muffled behind the t-shirt she was in the process of pulling over her head. She finished dressing, and then draped the skimpy dress she'd been wearing over a nearby shelf. She didn't care if she ever saw it again, or anything like it. Her days of being a high-fashion and swimsuit model were over.

"I know you have a bunch of questions, but Zachary is probably already looking for me, and I need to get on the road."

"But you just said you wanted to get unmarried," he reminded her.

"I do. What does that have to do with me leaving New York?"

"Brooke, I may not be a lawyer, but even I know you usually have to file for divorce in the same state where you got married to begin with."

Brooke looked at him, and then shook her head dejectedly, "So what you're saying is I need to stick around for another night, and file some paperwork before I can leave town?"

"I think so. If we can get someplace where there's a Wi-Fi connection, I can do some research on the subject, but I think you'll need to file the paperwork here." He didn't include that there was probably a waiting period she'd have to endure, as well. He didn't think she could handle any bad news right now.

And if Zachary finds me in the meantime.... "Fine. We can get a hotel room on the other side of town, and then in the morning I'll file the correct paperwork and we can leave."

"Fine. Finish up in here while I make a phone call."

"To Tyler?" she asked, her eyes searching his own.

He nodded, "I won't give him any details, but I need to let him know I found you, and that we're leaving New York."

Brooke watched him step outside, and softly murmured, "I wish I could go home."

Peter heard her soft wish, and decided right then and there that Colorado was going to be their destination. He didn't know what she'd gotten herself mixed up in, but he would do everything he could to help her get her life back together. He cared too much for her to do otherwise.

Chapter 4

Peter glanced at his watch, and then shook his head as he waited for the call to connect. It was almost 2 a.m. in New York, which meant it was almost midnight back in Colorado. He hated calling so late, but not knowing what the next few hours would bring, he wanted to at least leave a message on Tyler's cell phone, letting him know that Brooke was with him.

"Hello? Dad?" Tyler asked anxiously into the phone.

"Tyler, It's Peter."

"Peter. Man, what's up? Do you know what time it is here?" Tyler looked around the room as Trey turned the overhead lights on, and both women were now wide awake and listening in. Earlier that evening, both Trey and Tyler had asked the women in their lives to marry them. The annual Harvest Party had been in full swing, but the two couples had left before it ended. They'd headed back to Trey's house to watch a movie and snack on s'mores.

Seeing that everyone was waiting to hear what had prompted such a late call, he told Peter, "I'm going to put you on speaker phone. I here with Trey, Michelle, and Jenna."

"Uh...okay. That's fine. And yeah, I know what time it is. It's almost 2 a.m. here."

"What's going on? I've tried to call you several times. It keeps going to your voicemail."

"Sorry about that. You wouldn't believe the mess I walked into down here. I don't have time to go into all the details, but suffice it to say that your sister managed to land herself in a huge mess."

"Is she okay?" Tyler asked, rubbing a hand through his hair in his agitation.

"She will be. I'm going to take care of some paperwork on her behalf tomorrow morning, and then I'm bringing her home. We're going to drive..."

"Drive? But didn't you fly out there?" Tyler asked.

"Yes, and I'll explain everything when we get back to Colorado. We're bringing your sister's car and I figure it will take us three or four days, depending on how long I can drive each day."

"Peter, just answer one question for me. Is Brooke okay?"

There was a pause, and then Peter said, "She's not right now, but she will be. I don't have time to go into any more details right now, but if you want to do something helpful. Pray for her." Peter didn't tell her brother that he couldn't go into the details because she hadn't shared them with him yet.

"She needs all the divine intervention she can get right now." Hearing the roll-up storage door going up, he realized she was ready to get going. "Man...sorry to cut this short, but I have to go. I'll call from the road when I can."

Peter disconnected the call and waited while Brooke drove the car out. She left it idling in the alleyway between the rows of storage units. He helped her stash a duffel bag and his suitcase in the trunk, and then he gestured for her to get into the passenger seat.

"I can drive," she argued with him.

"Brooke, you're not feeling well, and by your own admission, you're not completely sober. Whatever is making you ill is still in your system, and, I'm not judging here, but I don't think you should be driving. It's also 2 o'clock in the morning."

She hid a yawn behind her hand and nodded her head, "Yeah, I know. Fine. I'll give you directions, and you can drive."

Peter held her door open for her, and noticed that she smelled like Brooke again. Ever since she'd entered middle school, she'd worn the same fragrance – a mixture of jasmine and spice. He'd come to associate the smell with her, but he hadn't noticed it on her in the nightclub, or in the taxi.

"Did you put on some perfume?" he asked, before starting to shut her door.

She looked up and blushed, "Yeah. Zachary didn't like me wearing perfume, but I found mine in my stuff in there and grabbed it. Too strong?"

Peter hated the note of uncertainty in her voice and shook his head, "No, it's you. Don't ever apologize for being you." He shut her door, and then walked slowly to the rear of the car. Someone had stolen her confidence, and he really wanted to teach that person a few manners.

FORTY-FIVE MINUTES later, Peter steered the red Mustang into the parking lot of a dilapidated motel in a part of New York City that he was sure wasn't safe or advisable. "Brooke, we're not staying here."

Brooke looked around at her surroundings, and nodded her head, "Zachary would never think to look for me in a place like this. If we stay at one of the nicer hotels, not only am I liable to be recognized, but you said yourself you, were running low on cash."

"I can afford a better room than this dive, and an ATM will fix the low cash situation in a flash."

Brooke sighed and then slowly nodded her head, "Fine. I don't know when I'll be able to pay you back..."

"I don't want to hear another word about money. Now, tell me how to get us back to a better part of town."

Brooke gave him directions and then grew silent, staring out the window as she thought about her future. She knew she'd signed over control of most of her money and finances to Zachary, after he'd convinced her that she didn't need the stress of dealing with those types of things. He'd promised to let his financial investment guru work on increasing her portfolio, and she'd let him.

She also knew that going to the authorities with her story would most likely get her a seventy-two hour hold in a local psych ward. Zachary already had at least one doctor in his pocket who would testify to seeing her in the throes of drug withdrawal. It would be her word against his that she hadn't been procuring the meds herself, and her former agent would only seal the case against her if he told about her using sleeping pills frequently.

Peter turned on the radio, and after switching through the channels, he finally came to a contemporary Christian station. Brooke listened to the lyrics of the song on the radio and felt like crying. The singer was talking about God's unfailing and unconditional love. She wondered how it was possible that, even after the mess that she had made of her life, God could love her. *Is that really true, God? It's been so long since I talked to you. I don't even love myself! How can you love me?*

"You okay over there?" Peter asked, sensing that Brooke was struggling to contain her emotions.

"Not really. I've completely messed up my life, and frankly, I don't really see any way out."

Peter reached over and placed a calming hand on her arm, "There's always a way out. Always. We'll find it."

"I can't expect you to just put your life on hold for me..."

"Brooke, I think it's only fair to tell you that I never stopped waiting for you to come home. I know a lot of things have happened since you left Colorado right after high school, but I still believe you're the girl for me."

Brooke said nothing for several long moments. She'd messed up her life royally, and she truly didn't feel worthy of anyone's love, especially this wonderful man sitting next to her. He didn't deserve to get the ruined shell of a woman she'd allowed herself to become. He deserved a woman who was whole, and not so messed up that she needed pills to get through the day.

"So, what have you been up to lately?" she asked, needing to change the subject, but her mind wasn't quite so cooperative. *Peter still wants me? But he doesn't know all of the things I've done. Once he does, he'll be sorry he came all this way.*

"I've been helping out with your parents' ranch." He paused and gave her time to ask about her mom's condition. When she didn't, he offered, "Your dad moved your mom down to Junction. He found a place there that caters to patients with Alzheimer's. From what Tyler said, their meals are prepared, laundry and housekeeping is furnished, and your dad has medical advice and assistance whenever he needs it."

Brooke still said nothing, so he pushed a little, "When was the last time you spoke to your parents?"

"Not since I left Colorado last time. Things here got so messed up and..."

Peter saw several signs for motels up ahead, and chose one in the middle; not a complete dive, but not a plush resort. "Why don't you stay in the car while I get us a room?"

Brooke nodded her head, and watched as he pulled under the eave and ran inside. Within a few minutes, he returned with a room key in his hand. Without saying a word, he pulled the Mustang around to the back of the motel, hiding it from easy view of the road, and turned the engine off.

Brooke was having trouble keeping her eyes open as more shivers wracked her body. She'd grabbed her spare cosmetic bag from the storage unit, and was hoping there was something in there she could use to take the edge off. Even if just for a few hours.

Peter insisted on carrying both of their bags, and she let him. As soon as they entered the room, she grabbed her duffel bag and headed for the small bathroom. She turned the shower on and stood beneath the scalding water as long as she could before getting out and drying off. She felt marginally better and she opened the bathroom door to let the steam out, having only wrapped herself in a towel.

When she stepped out into the room, she stopped at the look on Peter's face. *Gosh, I've become so used to having no modesty, I didn't even realize what I was doing.* Apologizing, she ducked back into the bathroom, and pulled on a t-shirt and a pair of knit shorts.

Peter had stared at her when she exited the bathroom, unsure of how to respond to her towel-clad body. On one hand, he knew she wasn't operating on all cylinders. On the other, he'd really seen no more of her body than if she'd been in a two-piece swimsuit. What had really captured his attention was the blush and embarrassment that had consumed her when she realized what she'd done. It was as if she was ashamed of herself, and that didn't sit right with him.

Brooke was a stunning beauty. She had raven black hair, deep grey-blue eyes that changed with her emotions, and a complexion that had at one time graced the cover of several well-known magazines. She was tall for a woman, reaching 5'10" in her bare feet, with a lithe body that had never shown a predilection for carrying excess weight.

She'd always been a beauty, but had also always been humble and not wanted extra attention. When she'd been offered a modeling contract, Peter had been surprised at first that she wanted to take it. But he'd also not wanted to stand in her way, so he'd stepped aside; assuring her he'd be waiting in Cathedral Hills when she came home. The problem was, she had never come home.

He glanced up as she came back into the room, towel drying her hair and muttering an apology.

"What exactly are you apologizing for?" he queried.

"I didn't mean to come out here almost naked. I really didn't, it's just...I guess I'm so used to not wearing much, it didn't really dawn on me to get dressed before coming out here."

"Explain that last statement," Peter requested.

"Well, for the last several months, four to be exact, I really haven't left the apartment, unless I was with Zachary. Sometimes for a photoshoot, and other times for an evening out, like tonight. Or rather, last night."

"Why did you never leave the apartment?" Peter asked.

Brooke sighed and then told him, "Peter, it's a really long story that goes all the way back to my time in California. Can we get into this tomorrow?"

Peter wanted to demand answers to his questions tonight, but he could see that she was exhausted and still ill. "Sure. You can take the bed closest to the bathroom. I'll wash up and be out in a minute."

Brooke nodded and grabbed her duffle bag, tossing it to the middle of the bed before crawling up and sitting beside it. "Okay."

Peter emerged from the bedroom a few minutes later, having brushed his teeth and washed up a bit, to see Brooke struggling to get the lid off a prescription bottle. "What are you doing?"

Brooke jumped, and then shoved the bottle back into the small cosmetic bag in front of her, "Nothing."

Peter shook his head and stalked to her bed. He pulled the cosmetic bag away from her, holding it out of reach when she made a grab for it. "Let's get something straight, right now. I'm going to help you, and that includes keeping you from hurting yourself any further." He dumped the contents of the bag out on to the comforter, sending makeup and other items scattering off the bed and onto the floor.

When the prescription bottle emerged, he grabbed it up and read the label. "Sleeping pills? That's what these are?"

Brooke nodded, keeping her eye on the bottle of pills, "Please give them back to me."

"Are you addicted to them?"

Brooke debated about lying to him, but she couldn't do it. Peter only wanted what was best for her, and the good Lord knew she hadn't been doing such a bang up job at that task herself. She swallowed, and then softly answered him, "I used to be, but I don't think I am anymore. They'll take the edge off and let me get a few hours of sleep."

Peter watched her eyes and could see how desperately she was trying to tell him the truth, yet wanting to hide it from him at the same time. "Brooke, you said you were suffering withdrawal symptoms. If not from these, then what?"

She shook her head, "I don't really know. I've been trying to wean myself off of whatever the doctor's been giving me, but I didn't know Zachary was taking me out tonight. I haven't taken any pills since early this morning, and then I only took half of one. I'm doing better, I really am. A few weeks ago I was taking two and three, several times a day."

"What's Zachary doing to help you get through this?"

Brooke huffed out a loud laugh, "He's the reason I'm going through this. He told me they were vitamins, and I was so loaded up on them and other pills, I just took them. He still thinks I don't know what he was doing to me."

"Your husband got you hooked on drugs?" Peter asked, incredulous, and thinking Zachary was a dead man when Tyler got wind of this. *The man had better count his blessings he lives so far away!*

Brooke licked her dry lips, "Please believe me; if I thought I could get through this without some help, I would never take another pill again. But I feel like I'm dying and I need to have my wits about me tomorrow."

"How many of these were you going to take?" Peter asked, looking at the almost full bottle of pills.

"Just a half, and maybe a couple of aspirin."

Peter held the bottle out to her and then retrieved a glass of water from the bathroom. He watched as she carefully broke one of the pills in half, and then placed the rest back into the bottle. "You know, for the last few weeks, I've been tossing the other half down the toilet." She laughed mirthlessly, and Peter felt his heart break for whatever she'd suffered these last few months.

She handed the glass back to him, and then snuggled down under the comforter. Peter picked up her duffle bag and set it on the floor. "Get some sleep."

Brooke closed her eyes, only to open them a few minutes later and ask, "Have you really been waiting all this time for me to come back to Cathedral Hills?"

Peter smiled at her and nodded his head, "I really have. Night, darlin'."

Brooke closed her eyes, holding the sound of his deep tenor voice deep inside of her mind, and hoping that it would be enough to keep the nightmares at bay.

Chapter 5

Peter watched her sleeping and then grabbed his phone, thankful that he had plenty of service and battery life left. He'd paid the extra fee to gain access to the hotel's not-so-free Wi-Fi signal. He quickly opened a web browser, and started researching the steps needed to get a divorce in the State of New York. Nothing he found was very useful, and worse yet, there wasn't anything she could do to obtain a quick divorce in the fine State of New York. She hadn't been married long enough.

He finally closed his phone and shut his eyes, needing a few hours of sleep before the day began again. He didn't know how long he'd been asleep, but Brooke's cries woke him up.

She was thrashing in the bed, having tangled her legs in the bed covers, and was slapping at imaginary things in the air. Afraid he'd get hit, or accidentally hurt her while trying to contain her arms, he straddled her body, and pinned her hands to either side of her head.

"Brooke! Wake up!"

Brooke struggled to free her arms, the things crawling on her arms and legs were driving her insane. She thrashed about, but something heavy was weighing her down, and her hands had become trapped.

"Brooke!"

She snapped her eyes open, and froze as her brain registered what her eyes were seeing. *Peter? What is Peter doing in my dreams?*

"Brooke!" Peter called her name a third time, seeing that her eyes were still clouded by her dream.

"Peter?" she asked, stilling her body and allowing her mind to come back to the present.

"Yeah, darlin'. That was some nightmare you were having." He slid off her body and released her hands, helping her sit up against the headboard. He walked into the bathroom and returned with a glass of water, holding it to her lips when her hands shook too badly to do the job herself.

"Want to talk about it?" he asked when she was finished drinking.

She shook her head, "Not really." She shivered and looked down at her arms, "I felt like I had things crawling all over my body."

"That must have been a pretty potent drug your husband was giving you."

"Yeah. I was really sick, and thought I was going to die when I discovered what was happening to me."

Peter glanced at the clock, and realized he'd been asleep for three hours. It was 6:48 a.m., and the sun was starting to come up outside. "Well, do you think you could go back to sleep for a bit?"

Brooke shook her head, "No. I doubt it. Did you find out anything about the paperwork I need to sign?"

Peter sighed, and then sat down on the other bed. He clasped his hands together and let them rest between his knees. "Well, I did find out some information, but not much of it was useful. You have to be separated from Zachary for six months to file a contested divorce; or if you could get him to agree to the divorce, you can file immediately, but it still won't go into effect until the waiting period is over. The court won't even consider your request until you've been married a minimum of six months."

"Great! He'll never agree to a divorce, and I can't wait around here for another two months!"

"The other option is to leave New York, take up residency someplace else for six months, and then file from that state."

"Guess that's what I'll have to do, then."

"You can file when you get back to Colorado..."

Brooke shook her head, "I can't go back to Colorado."

"Why not?!" Peter demanded to know. "Your family is there, and all your friends. Jenna's even back."

"Jenna's back? Wow!" Brooke was speechless for a few minutes, but the reality set in and she shook her head, "I would love to see Jenna again, but I can't go back there."

"You can and you will. Believe me, whatever reasons you think are valid for staying away are just plain wrong. There's nothing you can say, or that you could have done, that would make any of us love you any less."

Brooke felt tears spill over, "Don't you see, I don't deserve their love. And if they were ever to see what I let myself become..."

"Brooke, you have to quit judging yourself and assuming you know what others are thinking. No one back home is going to judge you poorly for getting used by a deadbeat like your husband."

"But that's just it. Zachary isn't a deadbeat. Do you know how I met him? I went to the DA's office to report what my agent was doing, and I got to talk to him. He protected me from Marco..."

Brooke stopped talking and dropped her head into her hands. *He's got me so brainwashed I'm defending him now! He is a deadbeat and a user and who knows what else. He deserves to go to jail for a very long time for what he did to me.*

Peter watched as Brooke came to the realization that she was defending the man who had not only gotten her hooked on drugs, but appeared to have been keeping her confined against her will. Lowering his voice, he told her, "Zachary is a deadbeat, and frankly, when Tyler finds out what the man did to you, he's probably going to be on the first plane to New York to set him straight on how to treat a lady."

"That's not going to help. Zachary Grayson's father was the DA for New York City, and then the State Attorney General before his death. Everyone loves Zachary and supports him, even if some of his actions are a little over the line. He has politicians, law enforcement, and even the Mayor working on his side."

"Well, then we go above his head, and get someone who isn't on his side to look at things. Who have you already spoken to about this?"

"Just Zachary. I figured the authorities were going to eventually catch on to what Marco was pulling, and I didn't want to get caught in the middle. I didn't realize at the time that Zachary was working with him."

"Zachary is working with your agent?" Peter asked, trying to put everything in some sort of order.

"I don't know if he was in the beginning, but he is now. I haven't seen Marco, but since I stopped taking so many of those pills, I've been able to concentrate and listen in on his conversations more. That man that was with me on the dance floor last night paid to be seen with me. After dinner, he would have had some professional photographs taken with me, as well, and they would have been used to promote his political career back in South America."

When Peter still didn't seem to comprehend what she was trying to tell him, she explained it in more blunt terms. "Zachary sold me to that guy as his escort for the evening. A few drinks, some food and some photographs, and Zachary would have received a nice contribution to his slush fund."

Peter was dumbfounded, and after a moment asked, "How long has this been going on?"

"Marco was doing the same thing to me. I found pictures of myself on flyers in his office, advertising my escort services for the evening. The ads were all in Spanish, but when I confronted him about them, he didn't even try to deny it. I purchased the Mustang with a bonus check a few days prior to making my discovery."

"And yet you kept the car?" Peter asked, wondering why she would do something like that.

"Things were really crazy during that time. I had gone home to see my parents, but Marco kept calling my cell phone and threatening me if I didn't come back to New York and finish out my contract. I changed numbers once I returned, but these men started showing up at my apartment, and I got scared.

"I went to the DA's office, hoping that if I provided them with enough evidence to put Marco and his cohorts away, I could get a lesser sentence for cooperating with them. I never spoke to anyone but Zachary about this."

Peter looked at her, and then realized there was much more to her story than her having gotten hooked on drugs. *Was she mixed up in some high class prostitution ring or drug trade?*

"I think maybe we should get on the road. I'm going to turn on the television and check the road and weather forecast, and then I think we should head out."

"I'm going to go take another shower. They seem to help with the withdrawals."

"Go ahead," Peter told her, grabbing the remote for the TV and turning it on. He heard the bathroom door shut just as the screen lit up, and he saw a picture of Brooke filling the screen. "Brooke, I think you had better come back out here and see this."

The bathroom door opened and Brooke came out, staring at the TV screen and listening to the morning news reporter –

"Brooke Grayson was last seen downtown around 88th last night, and went missing between the hours of 10:30 p.m. and 11:15 p.m. Her husband, Zachary Grayson, states she had been suffering from psychological and drug-abuse related symptoms for the last several weeks. He believes she simply walked away from the hotel and may not be acting with her safety in mind. She needs immediate medical attention, and anyone with information on her whereabouts is urged to call the number flashing across your screen immediately. A reward has been posted by Mr. Grayson, for anyone who helps locate his missing wife."

Brooke felt her body start to tremor, and she quickly sank down on the edge of the bed. "He's made it sound like I'm crazy and need to be locked up at the first available moment."

"Brooke, look at me." He waited for her to comply, and then he told her, "You are not crazy, and we are going to get you someplace safe. If you think you can forego a shower, let's get going right now. Does he know about your car?"

"I don't think so," she shook her head, "but if he checks DMV records, it's licensed under my name and everything."

"Do you have the title?" he asked, already formulating a plan to dump the car as soon as they crossed the state line.

"It's in the glove box. I know that's not the correct place to store it, but things were really crazy for a while."

"No, that's perfect." Peter stuffed a few things back in his own suitcase and zipped it up. He was pleased to see Brooke doing the same, and a few minutes later they exited the motel room and were driving away from the motel.

"Where are we going?" she asked, as he steered the car onto the freeway and headed west.

"Colorado, eventually. And I did listen to your arguments against going home; but right now, you need someplace safe to rest and recover. I can't think of a better place to do that than home."

Home! Brooke closed her eyes, and images of Cathedral Hills ran through her brain. She remembered the good friends she'd left there, and the fun times they'd all shared. Her parents were no longer there, but Tyler was, and she'd really like to see him again. *Maybe there was a way she could stop in and see everybody, and then just disappear while she got her life straightened out again.*

"No comment?" Peter asked, when she didn't immediately object.

Brooke shook her head, and then laughed when Peter muttered beneath his breath, "Good. Wasn't going to do you any good anyway!"

Chapter 6

Seven hours later, outskirts of East Pittsburgh, Pennsylvania...

"How you doing over there?" Peter asked, seeing that Brooke was finally starting to wake up. She'd been sleeping ever since they had jumped on the freeway leaving the city, cuddled up in the blanket and pillow he'd purchased from the motel when they checked out. Peter had paid more than three times what the blanket and pillow were worth, but when he'd really taken a good look at Brooke's face, he'd seen the dark circles beneath her eyes. He knew that she was beyond exhausted and sick.

Brooke stretched in the seat as much as possible, and then turned her head to look at Peter, "Thirsty."

"Hungry?" he asked, signaling to change lanes in preparation for getting off at the next exit. The signage advertised several fast food restaurants, as well as fuel services.

"Not really, but I know I probably need to eat a little something."

"Good. I'm going to fill up again."

"Again?" Brooke sat up, and then really looked out her window. "Where are we?" she asked, meeting his eyes.

"Pennsylvania. You've been asleep the better part of six hours."

Six hours? How is it possible that I slept that long without medicinal help? Deciding she wasn't going to question it any further, she gave him a sheepish grin, "Guess I was tired?"

"You're asking me or stating a fact?"

"Uhm...can I get back to you on that?"

"Sure." Peter steered the car off the main road, and stopped in front of a gas pump. "Decide where you want to eat. Burgers or cheap Mexican food."

Neither one sounded very appetizing to Brooke, but her stomach was already starting to object, and she knew some food would help give her body something else to concentrate on besides the lack of drug therapy. "Burgers," she answered, deciding that would be better than spicy food.

"Burgers it is," he smiled, before exiting to fill up the car.

Brooke folded up the blanket, and then set it and the pillow in the backseat before pulling down the visor and grimacing at her reflection. Her eyes looked wounded, with the dark bluish stain underneath them. Her skin color was so pale that it almost had a gray pallor to it, causing her to look more ill than she actually felt. The sleep had done her body wonders, and she noticed that her slight headache appeared to be gone for the moment.

"Still doing okay in here?" Peter asked, squatting down next to his open car door and gazing inside.

Brooke nodded, "Yeah, I actually feel a bit better."

"But?" Peter asked, hearing the unspoken word in her voice.

"I know that things will probably get worse again, before they get better."

"What seems to trigger the withdrawals?" he asked, wishing he knew exactly which drugs her awful husband had given her.

Brooke thought for a moment, and then shrugged her shoulders, "Maybe stress or getting anxious. I know after I would take just a half a pill, I would feel calmer and almost serene, like nothing could really upset me."

"So, maybe he was giving you anxiety pills?" Peter asked.

"Maybe. I know I was still taking the sleeping pills each night, and sometimes I'd wake up in the middle of the night and take another pill, so I could get back to sleep."

"Any other pills you were taking?" Peter queried, making mental notes so that he could relay them to the folks back home the next time they spoke. Maybe one of them could figure out how best to help her through her illness.

"No, I don't think so."

"Good. Let me pay for the gas, and then we'll go grab some food and get back on the road."

"How far are we going today?"

"Not sure. Be right back," Peter said, closing the door and jogging towards the payment booth. While waiting for his credit card to be run, he questioned the young man behind the glass about a car dealership that might be willing to trade the Mustang for something with better gas mileage. The kid eagerly told him about his uncle's place a few miles up the road, and even offered to call and pave the way for Peter's arrival.

He nodded to the young man, and then headed back to Brooke. After seating himself in the driver's seat, he asked her, "How attached are you to this car?"

"Are you asking if I plan on keeping it?" When Peter nodded his head, she laughed, "I have absolutely no plans to keep this symbol of everything my life became."

"Good, because I think we should get rid of it while we're here in Pittsburgh. If your husband runs..."

"Please don't call him that." When Peter didn't respond, she added, "I know, legally, he's considered my husband, but I was drugged up the afternoon we visited his judge friend's office and I remember signing something, just not what."

"You were drugged up when you got married?" Peter asked, developing a whole new reason to hate her husband. Sure, he knew he wasn't supposed to hate anyone, but some people did things that made them immensely unlikable. Zachary Grayson fit into that category.

"I don't remember much about that day. I remember we went to lunch and I felt fine. But during lunch, my head started to hurt. Zachary gave me a couple of aspirin, and then I don't remember much. Just bits and pieces."

"That might be important when you try to file for a divorce." Peter wished he wasn't having this discussion with her. Brooke was supposed to have married him.

"Maybe. You know, there's a lot about the last four months I don't really remember; at least, not until I found out I was being drugged and started taking steps to correct that."

"I'm proud of you for being brave enough to fight back. That took a lot of courage."

"Desperate people do desperate things," she offered back.

"Well, your days of being desperate are over. For good! Now, tell me what you want to eat, so we can get back on the road and find this car dealership the fine young man at the gas station gave me directions to."

Brooke gave him her order, and then listened as Peter ordered twice as much food for himself. She looked at his physique, and wondered what kind of metabolism he must have if he ate like this at every meal. He was definitely not overweight, and he seemed to have great muscle tone.

His arms were deeply tanned, and the muscles bulged beneath his t-shirt when he flexed them. "Quit showing off," she told him, thinking how much his body had filled out since they'd been in high school. Peter had always been in great shape, as had her brother, and all of the other young men. Working ranches, horses, and playing high school sports made staying in shape easy.

Peter laughingly flexed a bicep and winked at her, "Showing off? As if you'd be impressed. I'm sure you've modeled next to muscles much bigger than mine."

Brooke shook her head, "Not really. Most of my work before I came to New York was for magazine ads. Boats. Cars. Motorcycles. I was usually the only animate object in the picture."

"I thought you originally went out to California to model clothing," Peter commented, as he paid the drive-thru attendant and took the bags containing their food.

"Yeah, but I'm a little tall for most normal clothing. That became problematic at first. It seems that my long legs filmed better when I was wearing shorts or a swimsuit. I did a few ads for vacation spots and tourism campaigns, but mostly it was for large ticket items like speedboats and flashy cars."

"So, how'd you end up in New York City?" Peter asked, pulling away from the fast food restaurant, and leaving it to Brooke to sort out their food order. He took the directions the fuel station attendant had given him, and headed towards the car dealership.

"Long story," Brooke said, popping a few fries into her mouth, so she wouldn't have to expound upon that story right now.

Peter looked at her and then nodded, "Fine. But after we take care of the vehicle situation, there's not going to be anything but miles and miles of road ahead of us. I need to know exactly what's been going on with you, so I can help you find a solution."

Brooke sighed, and then reluctantly nodded her head, "I understand that, but I really made some poor decisions and..."

"...and what? You think I'm going to hold them against you?" Peter wanted to ask, hurt that she wasn't giving him more credit. Always, before, they had been able to speak honestly with one another without fear of judgment.

"Maybe," she hedged.

"Well, I may have put on some weight and filled out in the muscle department these last six years, but I'm still the same guy I was before. And I meant what I said earlier. I've been carrying a torch for you since you left Cathedral Hills, and don't think that you're going to douse that flame by confessing that you made a few mistakes."

More than a few. How about several years' worth all rolled into a few months!

When Brooke didn't respond, he reached over and touched her arm gently, "I mean it, Brooke. I'm not here to judge you. That's God's department, and I have enough to deal with trying to manage my own life. I don't need to go around trying to tell others how they should have done things differently. I may not like the situations you were involved in, but that has no bearing on who I think you are as a person. If you've made a few mistakes, then that is between you and God, and I trust you'll take care of the details when the time is right.

"I'm just here as a friend, and someone who happens to care about you and would like to see you smiling and happy once again." *He glanced over at her, and decided his short term mission was to put a smile upon Miss Brooke Jameson's pretty face. The long term would take care of itself, all in due time.*

Chapter 7

Taking care of the trade-in of her new model Mustang for an older SUV had been fairly easy, even though Peter was sure the dealership had made out like a bandit. He and Brooke had driven away in a five-year old Honda Pilot, with five thousand dollars cash in their pockets. Considering everything, Brooke was very pleased with the bargain that Peter had made. Since she'd had the title with her, the dealership had been able to process all of the paperwork right there, and the SUV now sported a temporary tag good for forty-five days.

"So, now what?" she asked him, as he headed back towards the interstate. She had her arms wrapped around her middle again, as she struggled to keep her tremors concealed from her very watchful driver.

"Well, I think we should probably keep going for a few more hours. The weather report said there's a storm coming down from Canada in the next couple of days, and I, for one, have no desire to be stuck on the highway in the middle of a blizzard."

"Me either." She grew quiet for a moment, and then asked, "Have you spoken with Tyler again?"

Peter shook his head, "He's been trying to call my cellphone for the last few hours, but I wasn't sure what to tell him. I also would prefer not to talk while I'm driving." *It's not that safe, and what kind of rescuer would I be if I saved her from her snake of a husband, and then got her killed because I was on my phone instead of paying attention to the highway?*

Brooke nodded her head and then sighed, "I guess I probably need to talk to him myself, huh." She shivered a little bit, glad that the worst of the nausea and tremors seemed to have passed. This time. She'd toyed with the idea of taking another half of a sleeping pill, but then she remembered the horrible nightmare she'd had the night before, and pushed that idea from her mind. Feeling awful was much better than waking up screaming in terror, every day of the week!

"That might be a good idea," he agreed, knowing that Tyler was probably going crazy back in Colorado, not knowing what was going on.

"Tell you what; let's drive for a couple more hours, and then we'll stop for the night. I don't know about you, but I don't have it in me to drive all night long." When she nodded her agreement, he asked, "You feeling okay?"

She relaxed her arms around her middle, and pasted a fake smile upon her face. "A little bit. I figure it might take a week or more before I feel completely better." *I hope it doesn't take any longer than that.* While she was feeling slightly better than, say, two hours ago, she knew it was only a matter of time before her body let her know it was going without whatever chemical substance it had come to rely on to feel good. She'd managed to hide her feelings of nausea from him, for the most part, and the only reason he hadn't seen her shaking was because she was sitting down.

"I figure that we can stop in Columbus for the night, and then we'll get started again first thing in the morning."

"All right," she agreed, wrapping up the rest of her burger and tossing it back into the bag. Her appetite was still very minimal, although the soft drink was just what she needed. She sank back into the leather seat and let her mind wander, as she listened to the radio and watched the scenery go by.

She kept replaying Peter's words over again in her mind, all the while trying to believe that they were true. He'd said that he hadn't changed, and that there was nothing she could tell him that would make him stop caring for her. As much as she longed to believe in that type of unconditional affection, that wasn't the way her world had worked. Not in a very long time, and she doubted that, when the truth was finally revealed, Peter would be able to stand behind his word. Not because he didn't want to, but because he wouldn't be able to look at her and not think about all of the things she'd done and allowed to unfold in her life.

Before long, she'd let the passing of the miles lull her into a semi-sleep state, and she finally gave into her exhaustion and let her eyes close. Sleep meant that she didn't have to worry about giving away how lousy she was starting to feel once again, and sleep meant that for a brief moment, she didn't have to try and come up with answers that just couldn't be seen.

Peter knew when she finally stopped thinking and went back to sleep, her body slumping forward in the seat and her head lolling towards the window.

He reached over and adjusted her head so she wouldn't wake up with a crick in her neck, and then he turned the radio down.

The miles rolled by, and Peter's mind was taking all sorts of crazy turns in regards to Brooke, and the people in her life who had been abusing her trust. So far, the list included her husband, her New York agent, and her California agent. He couldn't believe that there weren't others who had known how she was being treated, and yet, did nothing to stop it. In his book, that was just inexcusable. *This world would be a much better place if people simply opened their eyes and stood up for injustice wherever it occurred, instead of turning their backs and minding their own business.*

He knew that when things finally came out, there would be several people coming forward who would express thankfulness that her ordeal was over, because they had watched it unfold, and yet done nothing. They would assuage their guilt over not acting by making sure they expressed an over-abundance of gratitude for her rescue. Peter had no need for people like that, and he only hoped that she could be shielded from any more leeches in their small town. He already knew how he saw this playing out, and he also knew that Tyler would be of the same opinion he was. Someone needed to pay!

Three hours later, the lights of downtown Columbus showed up, and he took the highway past the metropolitan area and headed west. "Hey, Brooke. I'm getting ready to find us a place to settle in for the night. Do you have a preference?"

Brooke stirred in her seat, and then arched her back a bit and stretched. "Not really. Maybe someplace that has room service. I don't really feel up to going anywhere."

Peter looked at her in the waning light, and noticed that her skin had taken on a greyish tone once again, "You feeling sick again, darlin'?"

She nodded her head, and he hated the fact that he couldn't do anything for her. Not that she would let him do anything anyway. *Maybe after she talks to Tyler, he can come up with a way to help her that I haven't thought of.*

Peter pulled off the highway, and then into the parking lot of a well-known hotel chain. He didn't mind spending a little more on their room tonight, as he was going to suggest that they take it a little slower tomorrow, if she was still feeling poorly. She would be easier to convince if she had someplace comfortable to hang out.

"Hang tight and I'll go grab us a room," he smiled at her as he exited the vehicle. He entered the hotel and smiled at how clean and new everything looked; a far cry from where they'd spent the night before.

"Can I help you sir?" the young male attendant asked.

"Sure can. I need a room with two beds."

"Just for tonight?"

"Maybe two nights, I really won't know until morning. Is that going to be a problem?"

"No, Sir. That should be no problem at all. Check out is at 11 o'clock, so if you could just let someone down here at the front desk know if you will be staying beyond that, we would appreciate it."

"I'll do that. Does the restaurant offer room service?" Peter asked, taking the form the attendant handed him and filling it out. When it asked for the names of the occupants, he filled in *Mr. and Mrs. Peter Nash*, just to avoid any questions or misunderstandings on the part of the hotel. *Someday, the Good Lord willing.*

"The restaurant is available for room service until midnight. Here is your room key and a map of the parking lot. There is an outside entrance to the west of the building, and an elevator that will take you up to the fourth floor just inside the door. Your room should be just a few doors down from the elevator. Is there anything else I can do for you?"

"No, that should do it."

"You have a nice evening, then."

"Thanks." Peter pocketed the room key, and then headed back towards the vehicle. There were menus stacked up on a table outside the restaurant's entrance, and he grabbed one on his way by. There was also a stack of newspapers, which he normally would eschew, but a picture of Brooke, gracing the top right corner, captured his attention.

He quickly grabbed one of the papers and flipped to page ten, where he read a very touching story about a young up-and-coming lawyer in the New York City DA's office, whose lovely wife of only four months had gone missing. No determination had been made, as of yet, whether this was the work of foul play, or if she just wandered off.

Brooke was painted as being a flighty, slightly incompetent, model who'd fallen down the path of substance abuse, and her loving husband just wanted her home, where she could get the medical attention and care she needed. Peter felt like hitting something because of the lies that were being spread. The fact that the news article had made a national news sheet also posed potential problems, should they be recognized.

Placing the newspaper back on the stack, he exited the lobby with just the menu in his hand. *No need to upset her tonight. Once I get her in the room, there won't be anyone to see her until at least tomorrow morning. Maybe I'll have come up with a solution by then.*

He opened the car door, and then handed the menu to Brooke as he climbed back into the vehicle. "That's a menu for the in-house restaurant. Why don't you take a look while I get us parked?" It was a struggle to keep his voice even, but he managed it, for her sake.

Brooke took the menu and glanced at the various offerings, but nothing sounded even remotely appetizing. "Maybe I'll wait until after a shower before deciding. I really need to get out and stretch my legs." *Provided I can walk once my feet hit solid ground.* Her muscles had started cramping just before lunch, but she'd said nothing to Peter, not wanting him to postpone their flight from New York, and her past. They were still much too close, in her opinion, but a car could only go so fast, and they had been travelling for quite a while already.

"You can do that too," he nodded his head in agreement. "Or maybe we should give Tyler a call after we get up to the room, so you can quit stressing about it."

Brooke blushed, "Why would I be stressed over speaking with my brother?" *And why is it that you can still read me like a book?*

Peter gave her a look that begged her to deny his statement. When she looked down, he nodded, "That's what I thought. Tyler loves you, and just wants you to be happy and healthy. Trust me when I tell you he's going to be happy to hear your voice."

"I think maybe I should call him as soon as we get to the room." Peter was right, and in the back of her mind, she'd been trying to imagine speaking with her brother and explaining to him how stupid she'd been. He was not going to be happy with her.

Peter turned the engine off and then exited the vehicle, grabbing their duffel bags and escorting her inside the building. The ride to the fourth floor was quick, and moments later he was opening up the door to the room, and watching as she took in her surroundings with a smile upon her face. *Success!*

"Peter, this room is so nice!" Brooke slowly entered the small space, turning on several lamps as she moved around the spacious room.

"I like this hotel chain. I've never stayed in a bad one." Peter didn't often stay in hotels, but when he did, he liked to be comfortable.

She dipped her head into the bathroom and then gasped, "There's a jetted tub in here!"

Peter looked over her shoulder and nodded, "Yep, there sure is. Let's get your phone call out of the way, and then you can soak while we wait for dinner to come up."

Brooke took one last look at the bathtub, then walked over and sat down on one of the beds, "Okay. Can I borrow your phone?"

Peter handed her his cell phone, and then showed her how to turn it on, "His number should be the first one in the log."

Chapter 8

Brooke pushed the button to connect the call, and then realized that she was holding her breath. *Breathe! It's just Tyler, and you know he loves you no matter what.*

"Hello?"

Brooke listened to the sound of her brother's voice, and felt tears well up in her eyes. She had a lightning flash replay of all the times he'd come to her rescue when they were kids. *What would his reaction be this time?*

"Hello? Peter, man, what's going on? Hello?"

"Tyler?"

"Brooke?! Is that you? Where are you? Why isn't Peter answering his phone? What's going on? Are you okay? Peter said there was some sort of trouble..."

Brooke burst out laughing, as her brother continued to fire questions at her one after another. When he finally ran out of breath, but not questions, she hurried to get a word in, "I'm fine. We're in Columbus. Peter's been driving all day, so that's why I'm calling on his phone."

"Where is he? Put him on the phone. Brooke, it's so good to hear your voice."

"He's right here. I'll let him talk to you in just a minute." She paused as she tried to find the right words to say. There was silence for a lengthy period of time, and finally Tyler couldn't stand it any longer.

"Brooke, is everything all right?"

She felt tears fill her eyes and spill over onto her cheeks, "No, it's not. Tyler, I've made such a mess of things..."

"Are you crying? Brooke, don't cry. Where's Peter? Put Peter on the phone." Tyler's voice had risen and he was almost, but not quite, screaming his questions into the phone out of frustration. He hated it when she, or any female for that matter, cried.

Brooke handed the phone to Peter, and gratefully took the tissues he handed her in exchange.

"Tyler?"

"Peter! What's going on there? She's crying!"

"Yeah, I can see that. Look, she's in a bit of a mess." He covered the phone and asked her, "How much do you want me to tell him?"

"I don't care. He's going to have to hear it all sometime." *And I don't know how I'm ever going to be courageous enough to do it.*

He hated the resignation in her voice, but right now the only way to get her past this hurdle was to show her that Tyler cared for her, no matter what.

"Peter?"

"I'm here. Look, Brooke's pretty exhausted, but she told me I could fill you in on her situation; as much as I know, anyway. It seems her agent in California was working in cahoots with her agent in New York City, and they were using her to model for some foreign magazines with questionable morals. She was also being rented out as a beautiful escort, for those who were willing to pay to have their picture taken with her in public."

"What are you talking about? Are you trying to tell me Brooke was..."

Peter felt anger rise in him at the path Tyler's mind had taken. His own mind had travelled down that path briefly, but Brooke had assured him that all she was ever required to do was look beautiful and let these men put their arms around her, so it appeared as if they were actually with her. Nothing more had happened, and Peter had a sneaky suspicion he'd rescued her just in time.

Lowering his voice, he cautioned the man on the other end of the phone line, "Don't say it! Don't even think it! The answer is no, she wasn't, and trust me, she doesn't need to add that word to her already long list things she feels guilty about."

The sound of air leaving Tyler's lungs echoed Peter's relief, when he'd realized his thoughts had been wrong. "Got it. Did she not know she was being taken advantage of?" Tyler asked.

"Well, I don't know all of the details, but I can give you the short version for now. It seems she started using sleeping pills while she was still in California, and that led to pills for anxiety, and then stress. Her New York agent was taking advantage of her drug-induced complacency. When she realized what was going on, she confronted her agent and told him she was through."

"That was just before she came home last time. All of the phone calls she kept getting were from him, trying to pressure her to honor her contract. She changed her phone number, and then he started sending men to her apartment.
"

"She got scared and went to the DA's office to file a complaint, and offered to become a material witness, if she could get a lighter sentence when everything came out in the wash. Unfortunately, Zachary Grayson…"

"Isn't that the name of the guy she married?" Tyler interjected.

"One and the same. He works in the DA's office, and was the first person she told her story to. He took her under his wing and pretended to be her knight in shining armor, but he was really just another devil in disguise. Somehow, he became her new agent, and he upped the game by getting her hooked on other medications, but she doesn't know which ones."

"She's addicted to drugs?" Tyler asked, his voice lowering ominously. "Tell me you made him pay."

Peter glanced over at Brooke before lowering his voice yet again, and turning to pace back towards the entrance to the room. "Actually, according to the all-points bulletin he put out in New York, he seems to think she just wandered off. He has the authorities believing she's a danger to herself, and possibly others, and needs medical and psychological treatment."

"Dear Lord, what kind of people has Brooke been living with?" Tyler asked in a hushed voice, hearing Michelle come in the front door.

"Tyler?" she called through the house.

"Back here in the kitchen."

"Who's that? Michelle?" Peter asked, watching Brooke as she listened to him.

"Yeah. Listen, what can I do from here?"

"Well, you'll be happy to know that she no longer wishes to be Mrs. Grayson, but from what I could find out online, she hasn't been married to him long enough to file for divorce."

"There's a time limit on how long you have to be married to someone before you can divorce them?" Tyler asked incredulously. Since he'd never been married, nor did he believe divorce had any place in a God-directed marriage, it wasn't something he was familiar with.

"Evidently, there is. Six months. And if she's not living in New York when she files, she has to have lived in her new State of residence for six months before they will even consider accepting the paperwork."

"There has to be a faster way to wrap things up for her..."

"Oh, there is. If he were to go away to prison for more than three years, the court would grant her an immediate divorce, whether he agreed to it or not."

"So, she presses charges against him..."

"No go. I already suggested that, but she's convinced he has enough people in his pocket to make anything like that just disappear. He's already spinning the story to the national news, that she's a recovering addict with some mental issues."

"Well, there has to be something else we can do. I'll discuss it with Michelle, Trey, and Jenna, and see if we can come up with another way. When will you two be back in Colorado?"

"I don't know. If she's still feeling under the weather tomorrow, we may take it easy."

"Did you take her to the hospital?" Tyler asked. "If you need more money or anything, just give me a call, and I'll wire you whatever you need."

"We're good in that department. She doesn't want to go to the hospital, because she doesn't want any records showing that she had drugs in her system. She thinks Zachary would use it against her if he gets the chance. I tend to think she's right, but I have to tell you," Peter said, lowering his voice and stepping towards the window, "I'm worried about her. She's been going through all of the classic withdrawal symptoms, including tremors, nausea, and hallucinations. She's been trying to hide how ill she is from me, but I'm thinking we may stay put tomorrow; unless you all come up with another plan of action."

"Take care of her. I'm going to talk to everyone here, and see if anyone has any other suggestions. Please answer your phone if I call you again."

"Sorry about that, man. I was driving and didn't want to risk having an accident."

"No, that's fine. Don't answer the phone while you're driving, but maybe you could call me back on a rest stop or something, so I don't spend the day worrying about you both."

Peter laughed softly, "I get it. Big brother has spoken, and I will do my very best to make sure I keep you in the loop from now on."

"You do that. Can you hand the phone back to her, please?" Tyler asked, needing to hear her voice one more time.

Peter walked back to where Brooke still sat, and held the phone out to her, "Tyler wants to talk to you again."

Brooke took the phone, still wiping tears from her cheeks, "Hello?"

"Brooke, I was just telling Peter that, whatever you need from me and your friends in Cathedral Hills, you've got it. We love you, and I want you to know we've been praying for you since Peter called to say he had found you." He paused, and then added, "And we're not going to stop praying for you both until you're back home safe and sound."

Brooke couldn't stop the tears from spilling out of her eyes once again. *Safe sounded so good. But sound? Would she ever be sound again?*

Peter took the phone from her, spoke softly into it for another moment, and then closed it up and placed it on the dresser. "How about you pick something from that menu for dinner, while I go start a bathtub of water for you?"

Brooke nodded her head, trying to mop up the tears that were still leaking from her eyes. "Okay." Peter started to walk away, and she stopped him with a hand on his arm, "Peter?"

He turned back to her, and when she didn't look up at him or speak, he squatted down so they were on eye level, "Brooke?"

"I...," she looked up at him and faltered, not sure how to ask for what she needed. Looking into his warm eyes, she saw only acceptance and caring. It gave her the boost she required to ask for what she so desperately needed, "Would you hold me for just a minute?"

Peter felt tears threaten to steal his composure, as he heard the uncertainty in her voice. *Does she really think I could ever say no to a request like that?* Without a word, he stood to his feet, and then pulled her up to stand in front of him. Enfolding her in his strong arms, he tucked her head beneath his chin, closing his eyes when she laid her head against his heart and breathed a sigh of relief.

"You don't have to ask, darlin.'" He felt her arms tentatively wrap around his waist and squeeze him tight; almost as if she was afraid he would try to get away from her. "I'm not going anywhere, and any time you need someone to lean on, you can call on me."

He wrapped his arms around her, and said a silent prayer that he had been at the right place, at the right, time to rescue her. He'd never known a person more in need of being rescued than his Brooke. *His Brooke. She is mine, whether she wants to admit it or not. And this time, I'm not going to step aside and let her leave. She's coming home, and with a little luck, a lot of prayer, and a lot of love, she's going to realize that's where she belongs.*

Chapter 9

Cathedral Hills, Colorado, Tyler's house later that night...
"I'll get it," yelled Michelle, upon hearing the doorbell ring. She hurried to throw open the door, and greeted Jenna and Trey as they arrived with pizzas from the diner in their hands.

"Come in." She held the door open until they were through, and then shut it. The weather had finally taken a turn for the worst earlier in the day, and there was already a small skiff of snow covering the ground outside.

"That wind is cold!" Jenna said, removing her heavy winter coat and scarf.

"The weather sure turned awful fast," Trey commented as he took the pizzas into the kitchen, and popped them into the oven Tyler had already warmed up.

"Hey! Glad you guys made it," Tyler told him, shaking his hand and offering him a can of soda from the fridge.

"Michelle said you talked with Peter, and things weren't all sunshine and roses."

"That's an understatement. Come on into the den, and let's talk for a bit before we eat." Tyler led the way, and while the two women were helping themselves to cups of hot cocoa, he lit the fire he'd laid earlier, and then settled into a corner of one of the couches.

Michelle joined him a few minutes later, sitting next to him, while Jenna sat next to Trey on the opposite couch. Once everyone was seated, he shared with them the conversation that he'd had with Peter a few hours earlier.

Jenna was the first to break the silence, "So, this man Brooke married was basically keeping her a prisoner in his apartment, and drugging her to keep her unaware of what he was doing?"

"That about sums it up," Tyler told her.

Jenna shook her head, "That is wrong on so many levels, and illegal in every state! In fact, I think it's a federal crime. I can understand why she didn't want to go to the local authorities, but she could go to the feds. Especially if there might be photographic proof that her agent accepted money from foreigners."

"Peter said she seemed really set on not going to the authorities. She's afraid that Zachary will not only be able to find her if she does, but that any information she gives them will be used against her."

Michelle nodded her head, and then offered, "I have a contact with the Denver bureau. I could make a phone call and just test the waters."

Jenna looked at Tyler and nodded, "It couldn't hurt. She wouldn't even have to give them Brooke's name, unless it sounded like they could help."

Tyler hesitated, and then looked at Trey, "What do you think?"

"I think you don't have a whole lot of other options, and neither does Brooke. We can't just let this guy get away with what he's done."

"Alright, make your phone call, but keep Brooke out of it until you find out if he can help."

Michelle smiled, and then reached for her cell phone. Tyler stopped her, "Do you know what time it is?"

Michelle nodded her head, "Yes, I know what time it is. Believe me, Chandler doesn't work normal office hours, and he won't mind me calling him at 8:30 at all." She pulled her hand away from Tyler's, and scrolled down until she found the number she was looking for.

"Hey, Chandler. Michelle Cottrell here. Call me back when you get a chance. Thanks." She had no sooner disconnected the call when her phone rang. Picking it back up, she answered it casually, "Screening your calls these days?"

"You know it. What's up, Doll?" Chandler Hanson asked. He'd been working in the Denver bureau for fifteen years, and was planning to retire next month. He'd met Michelle years earlier, when one of his cases had overlapped with a case of child protection being handled by the State of Colorado.

"Hey, just a warning, but I'm sitting here with my brother, his fiancé, and my own fiancé."

"Congratulations! When did this happen?"

"Just a few days ago. Anyway," Michelle said, shaking her head, "I'm going to put you on speaker phone so that everyone can hear our conversation."

"Sounds like you've got problems?"

"Not me. A close friend. I'm going to paint you a picture, and then you give me your honest opinion about what she should do."

"No names, huh? Don't you trust me?" Chandler teased her.

"I trust you, but my friend has good reason to be wary."

"Got it. I'm all ears, Doll."

Michelle smiled at his continued use of the vintage term. Ever since she'd first met him, he'd reminded her of the old black and white movies, with the private investigator who went around solving crimes without ever breaking a sweat.

"So, this friend of mine kind of allowed herself to get hooked on sleeping pills and anti-anxiety medications. Her agent helped, and then took advantage of the situation. Money changed hands, pictures were taken, and her services as a photographic escort were even advertised. All without her knowledge."

"When she attempted to gain the backing of the DA's office, in exchange for providing them with enough evidence to make an arrest, she found herself at the mercy of a member of said office. That same individual, unbeknownst to this friend, took advantage of her further, making sure that she was at his mercy, and indebted to him by the use of emotions and fear tactics."

"This friend was also given drugs by this same individual, but was told they were vitamins, and in her drugged state, she believed what she was told. She was kept in their apartment, unable to leave without his escort. Her finances, and every aspect of her life, was controlled by this individual. He acted as her agent and her keeper. And he convinced her to marry him four months ago."

Chandler whistled, and then asked, "Your friend sounds like she landed herself in more than a little mess. Is this friend still living with this person?"

"No. Another mutual friend helped her escape the situation, but she is going through withdrawals from the drugs, and running scared."

"What State did all of this take place in?"

"New York."

Chandler gave a little whoop of glee, "Well, that's just fine. The head of the New York City bureau is a personal friend of mine. We went through firearms training together many, many moons ago. I happen to know that his team has been tracking a human trafficking ring operating out of the city for several years, without much luck."

"Last update I heard, they were almost sure there was someone inside the DA's office helping orchestrate things. Too many coincidences kept happening. He's going to want to talk to your friend. Can she get to his office in the morning?"

"No. I told you, she's running scared. She's on the road back to Colorado."

"Where's she at?"

Tyler leaned forward and introduced himself, "Chandler, my name is Tyler Jameson, and the girl in question is my sister. What good would talking to your friend do?"

"Well, first we need to get a blood sample analyzed, so we can have proof of what types of drugs he was giving her, and also get her any medical treatment she might need. Then we need enough information from her to get a judge to issue a search warrant for the place where she was being kept. From there, hopefully we can get enough material evidence to corroborate her story and arrest her husband."

"She's not going back to New York," Tyler told him.

"Well, hang on a second and let me think. If she won't go back to New York...we'll just find a way for her to give her statement to someone else who can be trusted." It grew really quiet on the other end of the line, and almost sounded as if Chandler had left the room.

Tyler looked at Michelle, and she just shrugged her shoulders, "He needs to think for a minute."

In all, eight minutes went by before Chandler and Tyler had a workable solution. Peter and Brooke were currently in Columbus, Ohio, but Chandler didn't have any contacts there, nor was he owed any favors from that bureau office. The closest bureau office he had connections to was in Springfield, Missouri. A bureau office that also had its own chemistry lab, and could run the blood samples immediately.

"So, I will contact Peter and have them head towards Springfield in the morning. They should be there before it gets too late into the evening." When he saw Jenna waving at him, he paused, "Hang on a sec, it seems someone else has something to add to our plans."

Jenna nodded her head, and then told him, "Remember, I told you my counselor friend took a new job in Missouri? Well, she's in Springfield! Peter could take Brooke there, and maybe Chandler's friend could go there to speak with her. It might be less stressful on her."

Chandler had heard the conversation through the phone line and echoed his agreement to that plan, "That works. He'll need to bring a nurse with him..."

"No, he won't. Teresa runs and operates a faith-based half-way house and live-in rehab facility. She has a nurse on staff twenty-four hours a day. If your friend can make sure he brings the right vials with him, I'm sure Teresa can find someone to draw Brooke's blood."

"Brooke? Is that her name?" Chandler asked, not having missed Jenna's little slip.

Tyler grimaced, but he answered him, "Yeah. Brooke Jameson, or...Brooke Grayson."

"Well, let's just see if her husband has people on his payroll working in the bureau." Chandler typed away on a keyboard for a few minutes, and then laughed, "Her husband is either stupid, or incompetent. He's been conversing with one of our undercover agents, and trading bits of information for over a year now."

"What does that mean?" Tyler demanded to know, afraid he'd just placed his sister in more danger.

"It means that Mr. Zachary Grayson has been frying his own goose for a year, and they are only waiting for another piece of evidence to come to light before they have enough to arrest the man, and put him away for a good long time."

"More than three years?" Michelle asked, remembering what Peter had told Tyler about Brooke's chances of getting a quick divorce.

"He'll be lucky if he ever sees the light of day again, where he's not wearing an orange jumpsuit and eating his meals off a stainless steel tray."

"Can't think of a better ending for a man like that," Trey commented, while everyone in the den nodded their heads.

Plans were made, and a few minutes later Jenna was talking with Teresa and letting her know she had guests coming for a short visit. Tyler decided to wait until morning to call Peter back, hoping that by now his sister had managed to calm herself down. Tyler didn't want to get her all worked up again just before bed. He had a very bad feeling that the natural course of things was going to cause her enough stress for three lifetimes before this was all over with.

Chapter 10

Late the next day, Springfield, Missouri...

"So, is there anything else you can tell me about these vitamins Mr. Grayson was giving you?" the FBI man, who'd only introduced himself as Mr. Black, asked. He was sitting in a casual living room, in a chair directly across from a floral printed couch.

"Not really. After I realized what was happening, I started trying to not take them, but I would get so sick, that I would have to take a partial dose of them just to keep functioning."

Peter had received a phone call from Tyler just before dawn, advising him of the plans that had been made. Columbus was well over an eight hour drive from Springfield, so he woke Brooke up, and they had been on the road again by 7 o'clock that morning. They drove straight through with only a few stops for food and gas along the way, and he could see the toll the long drive had taken on her.

The nurse on staff at the facility they had ended up at had already drawn three vials of her blood, and Mr. Black told her the results of her drug screen would be waiting for her when she arrived back in Colorado.

It had been agreed that returning to Colorado was the best course of action. The FBI agents in New York had been apprised of the situation, and the agent in charge was making plans to fly into Denver, and would be travelling to Cathedral Hills in the next few days to meet with her personally, if they didn't find the evidence they needed in her old apartment.

The agent conferred with the nurse for a moment, and she smiled and nodded her head before leaving the room. "She's going to get you some pills to help with the nausea and bad dreams. Don't worry," he assured her, when she started to shake her head. "Nothing she's going to give you is habit forming, nor will it have any side effects that you need to worry about."

Brooke tried to feel relieved, but she was still worried that Zachary was going to find out where she was and cause problems for her. "When will they be able to arrest him?"

Mr. Black smiled, "I'll be sending my notes to New York as soon as I leave here and can get them typed up. They should be enough for a search warrant, and the agent in charge has already promised to serve your husband with the search warrant immediately, regardless of what time of day or night it is."

Peter patted her shoulder, and then leaned down and whispered in her ear, "Everything's going to be all right. Are you starting to believe yet?"

She tipped her head up and slowly nodded her head, tears shining brightly in her deep grey-blue eyes. "I'm trying."

Teresa had watched the small exchange, and couldn't resist trying to offer this lovely young woman a bit of hope, "Brooke, I thought maybe you'd like to come sit out in the sunroom with me for a while. We could have a cup of tea and just talk for a little bit."

Brooke gathered her dark hair in one hand, and lifted it off her neck. The chills had given way to unexplainable sweats, the current one leaving the hair damp where it lay on the back of her neck.

She'd taken a liking to Teresa Martinez the moment the woman had first greeted her at the door to the facility with a warm hug. She exuded hope, and Brooke longed to have the kind of faith this woman did. *Maybe if I spend a few minutes talking with her, I can gain some insight into how she does it.*

Peter could see her hesitating, and urged her forward. "Go. Relax. I'm going to spend a few minutes with Mr. Black here, and then make a phone call to Tyler. I'll come get you when I'm done."

Brooke turned to Mr. Black, "Thank you for doing this so I didn't have to go back to New York City."

"No problem, young lady. I just hope we can put this guy, and anyone else involved, away for a good long time." He started to put his papers away, and then stopped, "Oh, I almost forgot. Chandler mentioned something about you wanting to ask the judge for a quick divorce?"

"Is that a possibility?" Brooke asked, not daring to hope.

"In these types of cases, as long as there is no evidence tying you to the crimes, the judge has it within his power, or her power, to grant you an immediate no-contest divorce, based upon the seriousness of the charges against Mr. Grayson."

"This case most likely won't go to trial for months yet. If you want, Chandler can have the agent in charge start the paperwork for the divorce immediately. It probably wouldn't become effective until the first of the year, but that's still a lot faster than waiting for months before you can even file."

"Yes, please. I don't want to be married to that man for one more day than I have to be."

Mr. Black smiled at her and said, "Consider it done. Go enjoy your tea."

"Thank you." Brooke smiled towards the doorway where Teresa waited on her. "Tea sounds very nice."

Peter waited until the two women were out of earshot before he asked the FBI man, "Did you get enough from her to put this guy away?"

"If her blood tests come back positive, and they can find evidence of the same drugs in the apartment, her testimony should help. If we can find some connection between her agent and husband, especially a money trail, it will be cut and dried."

"They won't let him turn State's evidence against his other business partners, will they?" Peter wanted to know.

Mr. Black grinned, "You've been watching too much TV. Zachary Grayson is definitely going to go down for this. The fact that he is so embedded into the DA's office will spark its own investigation, and if he has others working on the inside, it will be over for them as well."

"That is the best news I've heard yet. Thanks."

Chapter 11

"So, Brooke, I sense that you may be struggling with how to handle things when you get back around your friends and family," Teresa told her, after they both had their tea, and had seated themselves.

"I guess I am. Two weeks ago, when I found out what Zachary had been doing to me, I was furious. First Marco deceived me, and then I let Zachary do the same thing, only on a much broader scale. But then I started to realize that I let those things happen to me. It started back in California, and I let it spiral out of control."

"You were what, eighteen or nineteen when your California agent made it possible for you to get some chemical help?"

Brooke nodded her head, "I was nineteen, almost twenty."

"So, what experience in your life, up to that point, would have made you doubt that the help being offered wasn't genuine, and with your best interest at heart?"

Brooke stared at Teresa as if she'd suddenly had an epiphany, "I didn't have any experiences in my past that could have done that. I grew up in Cathedral Hills, where people are honest and, for the most part, always acted towards my best interest."

"Exactly! So, would you also agree that it's wrong for you to feel guilty over something that happened to you, and I did say it 'happened' to you. You didn't ask to become addicted to sleeping pills. You didn't ask to have your agent act without honor or integrity. You didn't ask to be kept a drugged-up prisoner by your husband, did you?"

Brooke shook her head, "Of course not." She realized that she was getting angry, and had to pause for a moment to make sure it was being directed at the right person. Mainly, her husband!

"So, what you're trying to get me to see is that I shouldn't feel guilty over something you don't think I had any control over."

"Well, you're partially right. You feel taken advantage of, and you were. You trusted the wrong people, and it backfired on you. Could you have stopped taking the sleeping pills before they became a habit? Sure. Did anyone in your life seek to help you deal with your insomnia in another way? No. And I don't think these are the things that are causing you the most guilt."

Brooke looked at her, and then dropped her gaze. *This woman sees too much.*

"So, would you like to tell me exactly what is causing you to feel so guilty and unworthy?"

"There were pictures…and my photo on advertisements for escort services…"

"And you're wondering what would happen if your friends and family saw those pictures."

"Yes, wouldn't you?" Brooke asked, blushing as she recalled some of the pictures she'd seen of herself.

"Most assuredly," Teresa informed her. "But, that is a real possibility, and you can't just hide away from society for the remainder of your life in fear that they will surface."

"I just feel so dirty!" Brooke cried out.

"There's a solution for that, you know?"

"God?" Brooke asked.

"Yes. He has the power to help you deal with this misplaced guilt you're carrying around. I want you to remember; those feelings don't come from Him. They come from the same one who would like nothing better than to destroy you over this."

"But how do I get rid of these feelings? Am I just supposed to pretend those things didn't happen?"

"No. That doesn't serve any purpose. You need to look at the situations clearly, and then ask for God's forgiveness over anything you did to knowingly encourage them. You need to realize that humans make mistakes, and sometimes they carry hefty penalties with them. You've been experiencing a penalty for trusting the wrong people."

"God's giving you another chance, not only with Him, but also with that young man out there. You two have history together."

"We were engaged to be married before I left for California."

"And he still carries a torch for you?" Teresa asked.

"That's what he tells me. He deserves..."

"Wait! You're talking about something Peter deserves, but what about Brooke. Doesn't she deserve something? Doesn't Brooke deserve to be happy, healthy, and whole?"

"I guess." Brooke answered her.

"I know. God doesn't want you to be unhappy, and spend the rest of your life paying for something that was mostly beyond your control. How well did you know Jenna?"

"Really well. Peter told me that she was back in town. I haven't spoken to anyone but Tyler, so I haven't had a chance to find out where she was all these years."

"She got caught up in the social work system. She used to feel just like you do now. Unworthy. Dirty. Not fit to be around polite society. But she was wrong, and so are you."

"How did she get past those feelings?' Brooke asked, leaning forward in her chair. She was so anxious to have some answers.

"She forgave herself for what she couldn't change, and then she asked God to help her with the rest. I'm not saying it was easy, and all sunshine and butterflies, but she's made it." Teresa paused for a moment, and then added, "Did you know that she thought everyone in Cathedral Hills had abandoned her, including her father? It wasn't until she went back to that town, and let people past her barriers, that she realized how much she needed them to finally heal."

"I think the same could be true for you. Peter mentioned that you weren't sure you wanted to go back home, but sweetie, you need your friends and family around you, to remind you of how special you are to them, and to let God remind you how much he loves you."

Brooke made a face and then sadly said, "I grew up listening to sermons about how much God loved me, but it's hard to imagine the same God who made the Earth caring about someone like me."

Peter had been standing at the doorway listening, and couldn't resist entering after her last comment, "Let me tell you about the Brooke Jameson you seem to have lost."

Brooke looked up and watched, as Peter approached her. When he drew close to her chair, he squatted down and took her hands in his own, "Such gentle caring hands. I remember these hands, as they bandaged knees and held the hands of little campers who were spending their first nights away from mommy and daddy."

"I remember this same person crying when, time after time, no one could find Jenna. I remember the nights you, Michelle, and Missy spent up at the church, helping Trey's mom and dad with one project or another."

"I remember the smile of joy on your face when you found out you'd been chosen as the Homecoming Queen our sophomore year, a fact that even the seniors had been happy about. Everyone loved your enthusiasm for living, and the joy you brought to everyone's life. You've been knocked down, but you're not out."

Peter searched her eyes, and then from the corner of his eye, he watched as Teresa slipped out the side door, leaving the two of them alone in the sunroom. He reached up and cupped her jaw, "Brooke, I know that in the eyes of God and man you are still married, but when that is no longer the case, I'm going to kiss you, and then you and I are going to have a serious discussion about our future. A conversation that should have taken place over six years ago."

Brooke heard the promise in his voice, and felt her heart speed up. Peter, in his own way, was staking his claim upon her heart. She wished that she was free to pursue that relationship right now, but their upbringing was strong, and she couldn't just sweep it aside. *I guess all of those things I learned as a young girl are still hidden down inside of me.*

"So, what's next?" she asked Peter.

"Well, Tyler informed me a few minutes ago that the girls are making threats to come out here and bring you home themselves. I'm guessing that was his way of saying he would like his sister back in Colorado. Pronto."

Brooke smiled, "Tyler's words?"

Peter smiled back at her, "You know it." He sobered and then told her, "He just wants to see for himself that you're really doing all right. You are, you know? What Teresa said about forgiving yourself for the things you had control over, and letting God handle the rest? That's the only way."

Brooke nodded her head, a small piece of her heart, and her faith, starting to think maybe there was a way back, after all. *God, if you're listening, please help me. I know I didn't make the best choices, but I let myself get caught up in stuff that didn't really matter. I turned my back on my friends, my family, and Peter. God, Teresa says I need to forgive myself...I don't know if I can do that without Your help.*

Chapter 12

Two days later, Cathedral Hills, Colorado...

Peter drove the SUV into town, stopping in front of the diner and watching, as Brooke took in her surroundings. Not much had changed since he'd been gone, nor in the six plus years since she'd called Cathedral Hills her home. Sure, she'd been home a few times for short visits, but she'd made sure she spent as little time in public as possible. *Now I know why.*

Brooke looked at the diner and could see people inside. Some of them she recognized right away, and others looked vaguely familiar, just older. "Why are we stopped here?" she asked Peter.

"No reason. Are you ready to go home?" Peter asked, seeing how nervous she was. The medicines she'd been given in Missouri had all but eliminated her bouts of nausea, and the sweats and chills she still suffered from occasionally. He looked at her, and could see a hint of color in her cheeks, and her appetite had returned with a vengeance.

Brooke nodded her head, and then leaned over on a whim and kissed Peter on the cheek, "Thank you."

"For?" he inquired, growing impatient to tell her about the phone call he'd received, while she'd been washing up during their stop for lunch.

"For giving me the chance to get my life back."

Peter grinned at her, "You are most welcome, darlin'. Let's get you home. Tyler texted me during our last stop, and I'm sure he's chomping at the bit by now."

"He probably calculated, down to the minute, how long it would take us to get here," Brooke said, knowing her brother well.

"More than likely. Uh oh, Trey just stepped out of the bank, and he was looking this way while he pulled his cell phone out. I'm guessing he's telling your brother we're in town." Peter put the car in reverse, and then pulled back out onto the street. He slowed down and waved to Trey as they drove past, seeing the grin on his face. *Yep, Tyler knew they were home!*

Peter didn't even get the vehicle to a complete stop before Michelle, Jenna, and Tyler came out of the house. Brooke threw open the door, and found herself pulled up into her brother's arms, and surrounded by two women she'd grown up with. Without even knowing it, she found herself crying and laughing all at the same time.

"Tyler, I'm so sorry," she told her brother.

Tyler hugged her tight, and then told her, "I wish you would have told me what was going on when you were home last, but that's water under the bridge. We're going to get through this. Together."

Brooke nodded, and then released him to hug both Jenna and Michelle. "Congratulations!" Peter had told her about both couples getting engaged during the annual Harvest party, and Brooke had been overjoyed to know that her brother and her friends had found happiness together. *Is that what Peter and I could have someday in the future?*

Tyler helped Peter grab Brooke's duffel bag, just as Trey drove up behind his vehicle. Jenna ran over and kissed him warmly. She walked towards the house with him, arm in arm. Trey hugged Brooke, and then shook Peter's hand, "Good job, man."

"Come on into the den after you get yourself something to drink from the kitchen," Tyler instructed everyone, heading there himself and tossing another log on the fire. Thanksgiving was only a few weeks away, and Old Man Winter had decided to bless the mountains with a fresh blanket of snow, dropping more than six inches in places.

A few minutes later, everyone was seated around the den, and Peter knew that he wasn't going to get a better time to make his announcement. "So...I had a call from Chandler when we stopped for fuel, just after lunch."

Brooke looked at him and frowned, "Why didn't you say something?"

"Because," Peter told her with a smirk, "I wanted everyone to hear his news at the same time."

"What news?" Brooke asked, nerves making her voice shake.

Tyler and Jenna were sitting on either side of her, and reached over to hold her hands, "I'm sure it's fine. Isn't it, Peter?" Jenna told him, urging him silently to get on with it.

"It's great news, actually. The agent in charge got his search warrant, and paid Zachary a little search and seizure visit around 3 a.m. two nights ago. They not only found the vitamin bottles right where you said they were kept, they found secret video tape that Zachary had been keeping of the apartment."

"What?!" Brooke cried. "He was videotaping me?"

"Yes, but before you start crying, that works against him. The agents went back a few weeks and saw everything, from you searching for a phone, to trying to leave the apartment and finding it locked from the outside. They've even managed to identify the doctor Zachary brought in the next day, and he's agreed to tell everything for a reduced sentence."

Brooke was stunned, still unable to believe that her nightmare might truly be over. "So, are they arresting him?"

"They already did. Chandler said the judge was so upset at his duplicity within the DA's office, she denied his bail and is holding him without bond until trial."

"Which will be?" Brooke asked.

"Three or four months. The FBI is still building their case, and trying to wrap up as many loose ends as possible. Chandler said to tell you that Marco is chilling, as well."

Brooke nodded but her mind was already making plans. *If Zachary goes to court in three or four months, that means I could be free of him legally soon after that. I wonder if Peter will still feel the same...*

"Brooke!"

She looked up to see everyone watching her closely, "What?"

Peter grinned at her, "Did you hear what I just said?"

"Uhm...about Marco..."

"No, after that. About the other things the judge did on your behalf."

"No, sorry. I was..."

"No need to explain. Let's try this again. Chandler is coming from Denver tomorrow, and he will be bringing some very important papers with him. First, the judge has ordered an independent auditor to review your financial matters, and she has promised to make sure all your assets are returned to you post haste."

"Secondly, she signed your divorce request. Given that Zachary acted in extreme malice towards you, and only used the marriage as a way to control and conceal his nefarious actions, she is ruling the marriage null and void."

"She annulled it?" Brooke asked incredulously. "Can she do that?"

"It's already been done. For a marriage to be legally binding in the State of New York, both parties must enter into the arrangement in complete control of their faculties. The doctor admitted that he began providing the narcotics to Zachary almost a week before the actual wedding took place."

"Brooke, that's wonderful news!" Jenna told her, squeezing her hand until it hurt.

Brooke looked at Peter, feeling as if she'd just been given the best present ever. *Thank you, God. I know I don't deserve this chance, but thank you from the bottom of my heart.*

Tyler could see the news had shocked his sister, and he suggested she take a few minutes to let everything settle in. "Why don't the rest of you help me get dinner on the stove?" Everyone but Peter followed him from the room.

Peter walked over and sat down next to her, picking up the hand Jenna had been holding moments earlier. "You're a free woman. You're no longer married, and there will never be a record that you were once married to Zachary Grayson."

She watched his face, and then reached up and pushed a lock of his hair back off his forehead. "That's pretty amazing news. It's so much more than I ever hoped for."

"God works in some pretty amazing ways. Now," Peter returned her caress, cupping her jaw and smiling when she tipped her head further into his palm, "I believe I promised you something once you were no longer bound to that man."

Brooke nodded her head, her eyes dropping to his mouth as she waited for him to kiss her. When he didn't immediately act, she couldn't help the request that spilled from her lips, "Please. Peter, kiss me. It's been far too long since you did last."

"Far too long," he agreed, dipping his head and lightly touching his lips to her own. Neither one of them moved for the longest time. They just remained there, with their lips touching each other. Brooke was holding her breath, but finally had to inhale, and that's when Peter deepened the kiss. *This is more like it!*

He kissed her thoroughly, not releasing her lips until they were both out of breath. "Wow!"

"Wow doesn't even begin to describe that," Brooke told him.

Peter kissed her softly once more, and then pulled her up from the couch and towards the kitchen, and the others, "Fair warning. I'll give you a month to get adjusted, but then I aim to ask you a very important question, and the answer had better be yes!"

Brooke laughed at him, "You can't demand I say yes."

"I just did. And you know what? In a month, you won't want to say no."

I don't want to say no now! "We'll see."

Peter gave her a sideways grin, and then shook his head at her when he realized she was trying to tease him. "One month."

Chapter 13

Chandler arrived late the next afternoon, and just like Peter had said, he had several pieces of paperwork for Brooke. The most important, of course, was the paperwork nullifying her marriage to Zachary Grayson.

His visit was short and sweet, and Brooke was thoroughly enchanted by the older man. "Are you sure that you don't have a wife somewhere waiting for you?" she asked, as he prepared to leave their sleepy little town.

"No. My work was my wife, and a hard taskmaster she was. I have several nieces and nephews though, and when I retire next month, I am going to enjoy spending the holidays with them."

Brooke smiled at him, "So, I haven't asked yet, but will I have to go back to New York and testify against Zachary?"

"Well, that depends on the judge who gets the case, and whether or not they agree to accept a plea deal from his lawyers."

"Is that likely?" Brooke asked, not wanting to hear that Zachary might be set free any time soon.

"No, probably not. The agent in charge is fairly certain that Zachary is the man they've been looking for. If they can prove that, he won't be given the option of a plea deal."

"What do they need to prove his guilt?" Brooke asked.

"They need to tie him to having dealings, and changing money, with any of number of South American bad guys."

Brooke was silent for a moment as she dealt with one of her biggest fears concerning this part of her life. *The pictures!* Taking a deep breath, she asked, "Would pictures of some of those people help?"

Chandler looked at her, and nodded his head eagerly, "Would they ever! Would those same pictures have you featured in them as well?"

She nodded her head, "Yes, I think so. Marco was advertising my escort services, and photographs to be seen with me. He had advertisements written in Spanish in his office the last time I confronted him. He's not the smartest cookie in the jar. He probably still has them lying all over his desk."

Chandler scribbled a few notes down on a piece of paper, and then grinned at her, "I'll let the agent in charge know. I believe they searched Marco's home, but not his office yet."

"Just…could you ask your friend to try and contain those photographs? To my knowledge, they weren't released inside the United States, and I'd really like to keep it that way."

"I'll pass that information along. It shouldn't be a problem."

Brooke breathed a sigh of relief and gave him a small smile, "I'm glad."

Chandler saw Peter come out of the diner, and he met him halfway with a handshake. "You take care of that girl there. She's been through a lot and doesn't think she's strong, but I've been doing this a long time. She's got an inner strength she's not even aware of. She deserves to be happy for the rest of her life."

Peter gazed at Brooke and nodded his head. "That would be the number one goal of my life right now. Shall I have Michelle send you an invitation to the wedding?"

Chandler laughed and slapped him on the back, "You do that, son. I'll just have to come back to Colorado to congratulate you both in person."

Peter joined Brooke, and they watched as the man drove out of town. "Everyone's waiting for you back inside the diner," he reminded her, when she would have stayed outside in the cold a little while longer. He rubbed his hands up and down his arms, having come outside without grabbing his coat first.

"You're cold! We need to go back inside," she told him, hurrying them both in the direction of the front door.

Brooke was greeted by warm hugs and friendly handshakes from the diner occupants. George was in his usual place behind the cook stove, and he waved a spatula at her, by way of greeting.

Missy was very pregnant, and waddled her way between Jenna and Michelle to give Brooke a hug. "I'm so glad you're back home!"

Brooke looked down at her stomach and then asked, "Should you be here?"

Missy laughed, "I still have a few weeks left to go. Or so the doctor tells me. Personally, I think this baby is going to make an appearance around Thanksgiving, but what do I know?"

Brooke laughed a little, and then was pulled away to receive more hugs and greetings. By the time she and Peter reached the circular table that had been reserved for their small little group of friends, she was laughing and relaxed in a way that hadn't occurred in years.

"So, what was the purpose for this little gathering?" she asked everyone at the table once they were seated.

Jenna spoke up first, "We're supposed to be picking dates to get married."

"Oh, yeah. I thought there was a specific reason we're all piled into this booth like sardines in a can," Trey told her.

"We all used to fit just fine, but then you boys went and developed muscles and stuff," Michelle told him.

Tyler leaned over and tickled her, "You happen to like my muscles and stuff."

Michelle kissed him on the lips briefly and then laughed, "Yes I do!" The air was light and carefree, and Brooke couldn't believe she'd given this up, once upon a time.

"Happy?" Peter asked her, seeing the light in her eyes that had been missing these last few days.

"Yes. I didn't realize how much I missed this camaraderie."

Peter wrapped an arm around her shoulders, and when she didn't pull away, but instead leaned her head back against his shoulder, he knew he was never going to make it a month before asking her to become his wife. No way would he be able to hold out that long!

His free hand drifted down to his jeans pocket, and he touched the small jeweler's box he'd tucked there that morning before leaving the ranch. He'd had that ring since the night of the senior prom; the same night Brooke had announced she was moving to California right after graduation.

He'd kept the ring out of sight then, but he'd already believed that God would one day bring her home and back into his life. *Thank you!*

"So, I know it's like only ten degrees outside, but I would love to see the old bridge after we eat."

All of the girls eagerly nodded their heads, and started chattering away about the times they'd spent on that bridge. The men looked at each other, and realized they would be taking a walk right after eating. The trail to the bridge was most likely covered with fresh snow, which would make it slick. None of them were willing to let their women make the trek alone, and without a big strong man to hold onto.

"I would love to join y'all, but this baby might be having other plans," Missy announced from the corner of the booth where she sat.

Everyone looked in her direction, and then spurred into action, "Thanksgiving, huh? That's still a few weeks away," Jenna told her with a smile.

"Well, either this baby's wanting to come today, or something isn't agreeing with...," she broke off, as another contraction stole her breath away. When it was over, she breathed deeply, and then looked towards the kitchen window. "Who wants to tell my dad?"

That spurred everyone back into action. Tyler went to get his vehicle and pull it around by the back delivery door. Trey and Peter took care of telling George that he was about to become a grandfather, carefully turning off the kitchen appliances and the gas that fed the large cooktop.

"I guess dinner's going to be at the hospital in Montrose," Trey commented, as he and Peter made the other diners aware that the restaurant was closing for the day. Immediately.

"Guess so."

Jenna came back into the dining part of the restaurant a moment later, "Tyler is driving George, Michelle, and Missy to Montrose. I told him we would be right behind them."

"We can do that. Hey Peter, do you and Brooke want to ride with us?"

Peter shook his head, "No. We'll be along in a little while. I'll stay here and double check that everything got shut down correctly."

"Good enough. Let's roll," he told Jenna with a smile.

Chapter 14

Peter watched them leave, and then he locked the front door and turned to see Brooke standing in front of a picture on the back wall of the restaurant. It was a picture of the girls, sitting inside the covered bridge, taken several years before Jenna had left them the first time.

"Remembering good times?" he asked, coming up behind her.

Brooke nodded her head, "Those days were so easy. Who knew how messed up life could get from there?"

"You all have had some bumps along the road. Jenna lost her mom. Michelle and Tyler just about didn't find each other because she was afraid of getting hurt. You had a few trials of your own." He was prevented from saying anything more when the sound of loud pounding echoed on the front door. "Let me see who that is."

Peter opened the door and saw a very athletic man sitting in a wheelchair, with a smiling woman standing right behind him, "Can I help you?"

"I hope so," the man said. "My name is Adam, and this is my wife Lorelei. We're looking for directions to Tyler Jameson's place."

Peter immediately smiled and shook both of their hands, "Wow! Tyler was expecting you last week sometime, but said you'd had some vehicle trouble."

"Just a bit, but everything's fine now."

"Good to hear it. Well, Tyler is currently on his way to Montrose so that Missy can have her baby..."

"Tyler's gonna have a kid?" Adam asked in shock.

Peter shook his head, "No. That came out wrong. Tyler is engaged to Michelle, and they are transporting a mutual friend to the hospital to have her baby. We were getting ready to head that direction ourselves, but I'd be happy to let you follow me up to Tyler's place. Stephanie's dad, another member of the community, finished the repairs and remodel, so it should be all ready for your arrival."

Adam nodded his head, "I still can't believe we're here."

"You're going to learn to love it, just like we do." Peter felt Brooke come up behind him, and smiled when she wrapped an arm around his waist. "Brooke, these are the friends Tyler was talking about. This is Adam and his wife Lorelei."

"I'm so happy to meet you. I'm Tyler's sister, Brooke."

"The fashion model," Adam added.

"Not anymore." Brooke smiled, and then looked at Peter, "I've retired."

Lorelei laughed, "Well, you're gorgeous, so don't be surprised if that doesn't last long."

Brooke liked these people, and she and Peter led them back up to the ranch and showed them the smaller foreman's house, where they were going to be living. Adam Landry had been injured while bull riding, and while the doctors hadn't been highly optimistic for a complete recovery, he'd recently started to gain some feeling back in his feet and legs; a good sign that his spinal cord was finally starting to heal.

"We don't want to keep you two away from the hospital. We'll be fine now," Adam told them a few minutes later, after Peter had helped bring their luggage inside.

"Good. You have Tyler's cell phone. Don't hesitate to use it if you have any questions," Brooke told them both.

"We won't. We'll be praying for momma and the baby, that both will be safe this day."

"Thanks," Peter offered, as they left the small ranch house and headed out of town. He took a detour, and parked in the small lot that led towards the bridge.

"What are we doing here?" Brooke asked in wonder, as she looked at the snow covered landscape, mostly untouched by human hands or feet.

"You said you wanted to see the bridge. Here we are. Come on, let's take a walk." He got out of the vehicle and came around to help her out. Together, they slipped and slided their way to the covered, snow-free deck of the bridge.

"I used to love this place," Brooke said. Turning a full circle, she held her arms open wide and smiled, "I still do. It feels like home. So many memories were made here."

"And plans for the future. Tyler and Trey remembered quite a few conversations they eavesdropped on when you girls would sit here for hours and talk."

"You weren't part of that equation?"

"Sometimes." He reached into his pocket and withdrew the small jeweler's box, "Brooke, I was going to wait to do this. I know I said I'd give you a month, but I don't want to waste a month, when I know my mind isn't going to change."

Dropping to one knee, he held the box up to her, opening it so she could see the ring inside. "I've had this since the night of our senior prom, and I kept it because I always believed God was going to bring you home again. I love you, and want to spend the rest of my life with you by my side. Brooke Jameson, would you accept this ring as a token of my undying love for you, and do me the honor of becoming my wife?"

Brooke looked down at where Peter held out his hand, and felt tears fill her eyes, clouding her vision. "Peter...I don't know what to say."

"Of course you do, darlin'. I already helped you out, remember?"

Brooke nodded her head, wiping the tears from her eyes before she looked down into his solemn face and whispered, "Yes." Her voice got a little louder, "Yes! Peter Nash, I would love to become your wife. You saved me, in more ways than one, and I know I don't deserve your love, but I'm going to be a little greedy and hang onto it."

Peter stood to his feet, slipping the ring onto her finger, and then sealing their commitment with a tender kiss. "You will never regret placing your trust in me. I will never take advantage of you, or mistreat you in any way."

Brooke clasped his jaw and nodded her head, "I know you won't. I love you, Peter Nash."

"I love you too, Brooke. How about we go celebrate a new baby, and tell everyone our news."

Brooke nodded, and then stood on tiptoe to kiss him one more time. As they made the drive into Montrose, she couldn't help but have a private conversation with God about the day so far.

God, I don't even know where to begin. I'm sorry for losing sight of what was important in my life, and letting it get so out of control. I'm sorry for the hurt my actions caused others, and I want to do better.

Thank you for giving me Peter again. He is such a blessing to me, and I pray that you would help me become the woman he needs, and that You want me to be.

Please, be with Missy right now, and help her deliver a healthy baby. Be with Adam and his wife as they adjust to their new surroundings, and please continue the healing process you've already begun in his life.

Lastly, I ask that you would show me what I'm supposed to do now. I can't go back to modeling again, and I'm okay with that. Show me what path you would have me take, and then give me the tools and the courage to pursue it. Amen.

· · ⚜ · ·

SIX HOURS LATER...

"The baby is beautiful," Jenna said, running her finger down his soft cheek.

Trey watched her interact with the baby, and then said softly, "You're going to make a wonderful mother some day."

Jenna smiled at him and said, "You know, several months ago, that thought would have terrified me, but not anymore. I will make a great mom, and our kids will know what it means to be loved and cared for."

Trey nodded his head as Tyler and Michelle came back into the room, "Yes, they will. Is Missy doing okay?"

"She's fine. George is going to stay with her for a while. I told them we'd go see what was happening here in the nursery."

"They were just getting ready to take him down to her room," Jenna said to everyone in general.

"Good, she's really wanting to hold him," Michelle said. Missy's delivery had been several weeks early, and her baby hadn't been in the proper position for a normal delivery. The doctor had felt it was safer, for both mother and child, to perform an emergency C-section, and both mommy and baby seemed to be doing fine.

Peter and Brooke walked in a few minutes later, and Tyler waved them to the door of the nursery, "That's him, right there in Jenna's arms."

Brooke smiled, and Peter couldn't contain his grin of happiness. Tyler looked at them both and then asked, "What happened?"

Peter tried to keep a straight face, "Your buddy, Adam, and his wife showed up right after everyone left. Brooke and I took them up to the ranch house and let them in to get settled."

Tyler nodded his head, but still wasn't satisfied, "That's not why you're both smiling like cats who got into the cream. What am I missing?"

Brooke raised her hand up, showing everyone her engagement ring at the same time. The women all cooed, although softly, in deference to the sleeping infants, and then the men all exchanged various signals with Peter, indicating they were on board and happy for them.

Brooke accepted a hug from her brother, and then the nurse was shooing them all out of the nursery to go celebrate elsewhere. They ended up in the waiting room of the delivery unit, everyone in their own way giving thanks for their many blessings. Brooke was no exception, and she bowed her head and thanked God for letting her once again be part of these people's lives. Cathedral Hills had been her home once before, and now it would be again. A blessing and a miracle all rolled into one!

Epilogue

Four weeks later...

Terrence Cottrell looked at the three couples standing before him, and couldn't contain his pride in them. Trey and Jenna stood directly in front of him, having just exchanged their wedding vows, and now sealing their commitment to each other with a kiss.

When they drew apart, they stepped to the side, and Tyler and Michelle took their place.

"If it's all right with everyone present, I'm going to skip right to the good part. That is, unless anyone here would like to object to this marriage?" When no one said a word, Terrence nodded his head and began.

"Tyler and Michelle, you have presented yourself before me, and this congregation, today to make known your commitment to one another and exchange wedding vows. May I have the rings?"

Adam leaned forward from his wheelchair, and handed the rings to Pastor Cottrell with a smile.

Terrence raised the rings up, and then closed his eyes, offering a brief prayer for their marriage, and then inviting first Michelle, and then Tyler to state their own personal vows. By the time they were both finished, there wasn't a dry eye in the small chapel, and there was still another ceremony to take place!

Tyler didn't waste any time after Pastor Cottrell pronounced them man and wife, sweeping Michelle into a deep bow, and kissing her until they were both out of breath, "Finally!"

Michelle heard his heartfelt statement and echoed it, "Forever."

"Move aside you two, and let's get this show on the road," Peter said from behind them.

He and Brooke took their place in front of the pastor, and exchanged their vows and rings as quickly as possible. A triple wedding was a first for the small town, but with the Christmas holidays looming, and none of the couples wishing to start the New Year still single, a joint wedding seemed like the best solution.

"Do you, Peter Nash, take Brooke Jameson to be your lawfully wedded wife? To have and to hold, in sickness and in health, for richer or for poorer, until death do you part?"

Peter looked down into the deep blue eyes he loved, and nodded his head, "I do."

He held Brooke's gaze as she was asked the same question, smiling when she nodded her head and repeated his vow, "I do."

"Then, by the power vested in me, I pronounce you husband and wife. Peter, you may kiss your bride."

Peter kissed Brooke, and then heard laughter as the other two couples joined them in another kiss of commitment. When Pastor Cottrell cleared his voice a few moments later, Peter lifted his head and grinned, "Sorry, Pastor."

Terrence just laughed at the three smiling couples, "May I present to you – Mr. and Mrs. Trey Cottrell, Mr. and Mrs. Tyler Jameson, and Mr. and Mrs. Peter Nash."

The congregation, which included everyone in the small town, and a great number of people from neighboring places, erupted in applause as all three men swept their new wives up into their arms and carried them down the carpeted aisle.

They went directly to a large room that was used for weekly dinners and get-togethers, knowing that their friends would be descending upon them soon.

"That was amazing!" Michelle said with a laugh, as Tyler set her down on her feet.

"I'm glad that's over," Peter said, loosening his tie from around his neck.

Brooke smiled at him, and then at everyone else, "I can't believe we all just got married!"

Peter grabbed her around the waist, and turned her in a circle, "Believe it!"

Brooke laughed, and then looked at her friends, "Did you ever believe we'd end up like this?"

Michelle and Jenna both shook their heads. Jenna spoke up, "I know Trey and I have talked about this, but do you remember when we were twelve years old?"

"Wow, that's a while ago."

"Remember how we used to hang out on top of the bridge and talk about stuff?" she asked.

Michelle and Brooke both nodded their heads, "Yeah."

"Did you know the guys were sometimes listening in? They would hide underneath the support beams, and listen to our conversations."

Brooke smiled, knowing where this conversation was headed, "I remember a discussion about whom we all wanted to kiss."

Jenna nodded her head, "That's the one I'm talking about. You were the only one of our group we didn't ask that day."

Michelle nodded, "That's because she was already head over heels in love with Peter, and we all knew they would end up married. I have to tell you, girlfriend, I don't think any of us figured it would take you this long to come to your senses, but I do think you got it right."

Brooke nodded her head, "I agree. Now, let me see if I remember how the answers to those questions went. Michelle said she would kiss Tyler, and I was suitably disgusted." She looked over at Tyler and told him, "We were only twelve, and hearing that one of your best friends wanted to swap spit with your older brother was really gross!"

Tyler laughed, "I was listening in, and heard the whole thing."

"You weren't?!" Brooke exclaimed, shaking a scolding finger at him when Jenna and Trey both nodded their heads. Placing her hands on her hips, she glared at her brother, "Just how many times did you guys sneak around and listen to us?"

Tyler shook his head, "Guess you'll never know."

Michelle laughed at her disgruntled look, glad to finally start seeing the friend she knew coming back. Brooke had always been the life of their little group, and she had really missed her presence in their lives. "Well, I remember Jenna's answer."

Jenna blushed, and then laughed, "I'm not going to feel badly about my answer. He married me, didn't he? And now I can kiss him any time I want to."

Trey grabbed her around the waist and kissed her before replying, "Same goes for me."

Brooke looked around her, and then grew sober, "We're quite a crew. Life pulled us in so many directions, some of us trying our best to mess things up, and yet here we all are."

"God knew what he was doing when he brought us all together as kids. I think it's one of the greatest things about being human. Knowing that God lets us make our mistakes, just waiting in the wings for us to realize we've strayed and need His help."

"I sure wish He would have intervened a little sooner in some instances," Jenna said, with Brooke nodding her head.

"Do you really?" Mary Cottrell said, as she entered the small reception hall with her husband. She'd heard the conversation, and hadn't been able to resist interjecting some wisdom into it.

"Think about where your lives have taken you, and the lessons you've learned. Jenna, your teen years were horrible, and while we wouldn't wish those experiences on anyone, you fought back and won the victory. Those experiences are going to guide you, and help you protect other kids from having to ever go through them; kids that might not have the benefit of friends and family, and a relationship with God to pull them back from harm's reach.

"And Michelle. Your work inside the system has already proven useful in helping Peter track down Brooke and bring her home. Your knowledge of how the system works, and your counseling experience, combined with Jenna's, is going to save lots of young lives."

She walked over and hugged Brooke, "I know you feel adrift right now, but trust me when I tell you that God has something mighty planned for your life. He hasn't shown it to you yet, but He will. Your experiences will be helpful, as well."

Mary looked at each of the young men standing before her. "Trey, my son, I am so proud of the man you've become. God has placed you in a position to help secure and manage the finances of the operation Jenna wants to set up. I know God is going to bless your efforts.

"Tyler, I met your riding partner and his wife, and I don't believe it's a coincidence that he was injured at this time, or that you were able to move back home. God has mighty things in store for you all, just keep following where He leads you."

"Peter, God always needs a willing warrior, ready to fight. That is what I see when I look at you. Your loyalty to Brooke for all these years has been amazing to witness, and I pray that God will continue to bless you with the desires of your heart."

"He already has, Mrs. Cottrell," Peter told her, pulling Brooke close to his side once again.

"I think I can speak for all of us, Mom, when I say that we all feel blessed beyond measure. Cathedral Hills is a special place, and because of people like you and dad, it's a place we can truly call home."

Everyone nodded their head as the doors opened and their guests started to file in. Peter pulled Brooke with him, and then gestured for the other two couples to join him, as they slipped into the small kitchen.

"What's up?" Trey asked, wrapping his arms around his new wife from behind.

Peter looked at them all, "I just wanted to say how much I admire each one of you, and from this day forward, we are all connected."

Tyler nodded his head, resting his chin on Michelle's head, "I agree. We've been friends and family for a long time; but now we have a special bond to help each other and nurture each other as we become parents and leaders in this community."

Jenna looked around at each person and then, with tears in her eyes, she said, "Cathedral Hills saved me. I thought it had destroyed me, but I was wrong. The bonds that are formed here last a lifetime, and not tragedy, or deception, or evil can take away what we have here. I can't wait to see what God has in store for the next generation."

All six heads nodded in agreement, as Trey closed his eyes and offered up a prayer for them all, "God, thank you for the people standing in this room. May we be accountable to each other, and to You as we step into the next phase of our lives. Bless us so that we may bless others, and for those amongst us who are still searching for answers, we pray that you would let them feel the happiness we do right now. Amen."

As they headed back out to greet their guests, they didn't do it as an abandoned teen, or a fearful and heartbroken young adult, or as a drug-addicted, mindless slave. They went out as the warrior, ready to fight for justice in the lives of abandoned children; as the loving woman who had seen tragedy, and come out the other side stronger and more determined than ever to fight for what was right; and as a young woman who finally knew that everything she ever wanted was right here at home. Joy wasn't to be found in the accolades of strangers, or money in the bank. Joy was knowing you were loved and accepted by people who could laugh and cry with you, and tell you the truth, even when you didn't want to hear it. Joy was here – in Cathedral Hills!

DID YOU LOVE *Brooke and Peter*? Then you should read the complete set of all 3 books in *Home To You Series* by Morris Fenris. Below, you can read a sample of Book 1, *No Place Like Home*.

CHAPTER 1

Wednesday, December 12th
Central Mountains of Wyoming

Jerricha Ballard, known to her adoring fans as the lead singer for the pop band, *Jericho*, yawned and struggled to see the road sign up ahead. She'd been driving for what felt like two years, but in reality, it had only been for the last two days. She and her traveling partner had spent last night in a small motel, in an even smaller town, paid for in cash. She smiled as she recalled feeling like a criminal on the run as she'd paid for the room and accepted the well-worn key.

She turned the windshield wipers up a notch, trying to clear the rapidly falling snow, but it didn't really seem to help. It was December in Wyoming and she'd been driving in this storm for the last six hours. It was taking a toll on her concentration.

"Does it snow here all winter long?" a voice whined from the passenger seat. "*Brr*. I've never been so cold in my life."

"What did you expect, Cass? Palm trees and sand? This is Wyoming, after all." Jerricha risked a glance at her best friend, Cassidy Peters.

The tires hit a patch of ice and their massive truck slid. Jerricha gripped the steering wheel and corrected its course, peering into the storm.

"Whoa! Take it easy," Cassidy warned her, grabbing the bar above the passenger door. "We've made it this far, don't land us in a ditch now."

Jerricha grimaced, "I've been driving in snow like this since I was sixteen. I can handle it."

"I didn't say you couldn't, but if you wreck Ben's truck, he's going to be doubly ticked off."

Ben Morgan was Jerricha's manager and producer all wrapped into one package. He abhorred traveling on the tour bus and instead chose to drive himself from venue to venue. Jerricha's last three albums had gone platinum, and with the percentage she paid Ben, he'd more than been able to afford the fifty-thousand-dollar truck she'd *borrowed* two nights ago.

"Ben will be fine," Jerricha stated, a note of wishful thinking making its way into her voice. *He's going to be furious with me! Maybe so mad he'll actually make good on his threat to not represent me anymore. That would be such a shame.* She shook her head at the sarcastic thoughts running through her mind and returned her attention to the rapidly deteriorating road conditions.

Cass released a rueful laugh. "That's why he's called over a hundred times in the last two days. Because he knows you're taking such good care of his baby." His baby being the cherry red, double cab, Ford F-350 truck with the lift kit, chrome everything, leather seats, and more amenities than any one person really needs in a vehicle.

"We haven't hurt his precious truck and I even texted him a picture of it at breakfast this morning to prove it."

"Did you tell him where we were?"

"I'm not stupid. Of course not. If I had, he'd have made up some story to get the State Police involved and we would not be almost there now."

Cass looked out the window at the snow-covered landscape and frowned. "Where exactly is it we're going? All I see are mountains and more mountains, and snow. Lots and lots of snow."

"We're headed to Warm Springs, Wyoming," Jerricha replied, relieved when she saw a new road sign up ahead, indicating they were only thirty miles from their destination.

"Warm Springs? What's there?" Cass asked. She'd become best friends with Jerricha several years ago and now went practically everywhere with her. She handled her phone calls, managed the adoring fans always wanting a meet and greet with their favorite pop singer, and, when things got overwhelming, she was the last line of defense between Jerricha and everyone else. Even Ben. Cassidy was the sister Jerricha had never had.

Jerricha nodded, replying softly, "It's where I spent my teenage years. I haven't been here in almost a year. The last time... well, suffice it to say, I could have done without coming back to bury my aunt. Remember last year when I disappeared for two days and everyone was speculating that I'd checked myself into a rehab facility?" When Cassidy nodded, Jerricha grinned. "I came here."

She and Ben had created an elaborate diversion for the press, which had allowed her to travel to Warm Springs for the funeral and fly right back out when it was over. She'd not even been in the town forty-eight hours, something she still regretted. The media had taken the opportunity to speculate, just as she assumed they were doing now. She and Cassidy had made an agreement not to turn on the news or check their social media until they'd reached their destination. Jerricha was taking this time for herself and she wouldn't let anything interfere with her enjoyment of it. She'd missed this place. It was the closest thing she had to a home.

In reality, she'd not been home more often because she refused to subject the town of Warm Springs and her family to the madness her popularity brought. Instead, she and her family kept in touch via video chatting and once in a while she had flown her aunt, uncle, and cousins to a remote vacation destination where photographers and the press were not allowed. But that was before her aunt had suffered a massive stroke that had taken her life a week later. There would be no more family trips. Not for a while. Maybe not ever.

So instead, Jerricha was coming to them this year. The only reason why there wasn't a line of reporters following them now was because she and Cass had skipped out of her Kansas City concert while fans had been screaming for an encore performance.

The band had expected Jerricha to come back onstage, as well, but instead, Cass had snatched Ben's truck keys, packed some of their clothing up during the first half of the concert and tucked their luggage away inside the truck. She'd been waiting for Jerricha at the delivery entrance of the stadium. They were on the highway headed West before anyone had caught on.

They'd stopped at an all-night truck stop on the outskirts of Kansas City and Jerricha had removed the purple streaks from her hair, pulled out the hair extensions, and changed into a pair of well-worn jeans, a flannel shirt over a tank top that she'd had since high school, and a pair of snow boots.

She glanced over at her friend and once again could only shake her head in disbelief. She'd told Cassidy they were heading into the mountains in the middle of the winter, but that evidently hadn't meant much to the city-bred girl from Miami. Cassidy had abandoned her torn leggings, mini skirt and halter top, but her choice of alternate attire wasn't quite what Jerricha had in mind. Cassidy currently wore leather pants, and a bulky sweater with a bright red bra showing through the wide weave pattern. Her hair still sported multi-colored stripes, and her ears and neck were still adorned with lots of jewelry. She would stick out like a sore thumb in Warm Springs. *I'll have to get her some proper clothing as soon as we get there. She's liable to scare half the town dressed this way.*

"So, is all of your family still in Warm Springs?" Cass asked, oblivious to Jerricha's thoughts on her behalf.

Jerricha shook her head. "Not all of them. My parents still live there, and I have an aunt and uncle there in the summer months. They spend the rest of the year in Florida, playing golf."

"Florida. Now that's where we should have gone. Plenty of palm trees, ocean, and tanned guys."

Jerricha chuckled and shook her head. "It's almost Christmas. I haven't been able to spend Christmas in Warm Springs since I was nineteen. That changes this year."

"You must really love this place. But I don't get it. You've never really talked about your childhood. In fact, I don't even know if you have siblings. Why is that?"

Jerricha gave her an incredulous look. "You've fought off the cameras and microphones right alongside me and you can ask that? I don't talk about my hometown because this is mine. I don't want it destroyed by the media and their constant lies."

"I can understand that, but you know it's only a matter of time before someone finds out and comes here looking for you. You can't just disappear without a trace and expect people to let it go."

"I don't have another concert scheduled until after the first of next year. No one will be looking for me. And I hardly look like the lead singer from *Jericho*. Even if they come looking, they won't be looking for a mountain girl with normal hair, no tattoos, and no makeup on." *I hope. Maybe I should call Ben and make sure he's running interference for me.*

"You're thinking of calling Ben," Cass said, watching her carefully.

Jerricha nodded. "I probably need to, but..."

"But..."

"He does know where I'm from and if he thinks this is where I've gone, he won't hesitate to come here and that would be a disaster. I'll call him when we get there."

"What are you going to say?" Cassidy asked with wide eyes.

Jerricha shrugged. "I have no idea. Maybe I'll just tell him I quit." At the look of horror on Cassidy's face, Jerricha sighed and then told her, "I'll figure something out. Don't worry. As for siblings, I have two brothers. Kaedon is four years older than me and runs a construction company that specializes in restoring old homes and such. He travels quite a bit, but he still has a home in Warm Springs. Rylor is a social worker in Cheyenne."

"Wow. Two brothers. I never knew that. Like I said, you rarely talk about your family."

Jerricha smiled, deciding to keep the fact that Rylor was also her twin a secret for now. Instead, she replied, "I've gotten so used to keeping my personal life a secret, not even the band members know about my personal life."

"Afraid they'll talk to the wrong person?"

Jerricha nodded. "You know it. The band was put together by the record label when I was nineteen. We seemed to all work together really well in the early days and before we knew it, the band was a success."

"Yeah, but don't you think your fans will get tired of you all refusing to give interviews and do the award shows?"

"Maybe, but given that our last record went platinum in the first week, I'm not really buying into the panic that Ben likes to peddle. A little mystery surrounding myself and the band members keeps people interested."

"Yeah, well, one of these days your little secret is going to get out. What then?"

"I'll cross that bridge when I come to it. Besides, who knows how much longer the band will be together? In case you haven't noticed, some of the band members don't exactly exude high morals."

Cassidy grimaced. "I've noticed. So has the rest of the world."

"Yeah, I'm getting tired of hearing Ben yell about legal fees and such. I wish they'd all just settle down and stop acting out."

"Maybe this is just a phase they're going through," Cassidy offered.

"Maybe." Jerricha turned her attention back to the road. The snowdrifts on the road's sides were a testament to how much snow had fallen in recent days. It was still coming down strong and she was anxious to get to town and off the roads before the storm got any worse. She was anxious to see her parents and start relaxing. It had been way too many months since she'd even thought about doing nothing and the idea was really appealing. *Almost home. Just a few more miles.*

Chapter 2

"So…," Cassidy drew the word out and then changed the subject. "Don't the townsfolk know who you are and why haven't they told anyone?"

Jerricha smiled at Cass. "You've never met the people of Warm Springs. They protect their own and they hate reporters. Years ago, a man from Warm Springs, Godfrey Merkel, decided he could do a better job as governor than the current man sitting in Cheyenne and he ran for office. The reporters descended on the town with their news trucks and lights… It quickly turned into a circus."

"I can see why that might have been annoying to the townsfolk, but hate? That seems a little strong."

"It's not. The reporters were so intent on digging up dirt on the man, nothing was off limits. They completely took over the town. They parked their trucks wherever, were constantly asking everyone questions, and left a trail of destruction behind them. The final straw was when one of the news trucks' drivers, arriving late at night, thought he'd found a nice vacant patch of grass to park his truck on for the night."

"What he'd do, wind up in the city park?" Cass asked.

Jerricha shook her head. "Much worse. He was parked in the cemetery, right on top of the would-be governor's late wife's grave. The press had been in town for a week, and everyone was sick and tired of the hoopla they created. Desecrating the cemetery was the final straw.

"The sheriff, along with half a dozen men from town, had had enough and ran every last media person and photographer out of town."

"Didn't they just come right back?" Cass had witnessed firsthand how tenacious the press could be.

"They tried, but there's only one road into and out of Warm Springs. The sheriff and men from town set up a blockade and then manned it, armed with rifles. He even deputized them to make it all legal and such. After a few days, everyone gave up and they never came back."

"What happened to the man who wanted to be governor?"

"Godfrey? Well, he decided that level of politics wasn't for him and when the position of mayor became available, he ran and won. He's been mayor ever since."

"But how does that keep you protected?" Cassidy wanted to know.

"It just does. Not everyone knows who I am and those that do... they guard my secret very closely. You said it yourself. No one would recognize me if I'm dressed like this."

"But the minute you open your mouth and sing anything, everyone will know exactly who you are," Cassidy argued.

Jerricha's throaty, raspy voice was her trademark sound and easily recognizable by anyone who listened to popular music. "I'll just have to keep my singing relegated to the showers then, won't I?"

Cassidy chuckled and shook her head. "I'll believe that when I see it." Jerricha's life was one big song. She ate, slept, and breathed music of one sort or another. "I bet I catch you singing in the first twenty-hours we're here."

"Maybe, but I'm certain my secret is safe here. You'll understand that once you meet some of the townsfolk. Nicer people don't exist on the planet."

Jerricha put on her blinker and slowly navigated the turn onto the road leading to her hometown. The place where she could be herself. Her sanctuary. The one place in the world where she could count on being accepted for who she was as a person, not as a celebrity.

"Cass, I hate to ask this, but it's kind of necessary. We need to turn our cell phones completely off. You can turn it back on whenever you need to make a call, but I wouldn't put it past Ben to try and track our phones and I just want to be alone for a while."

"Hey, you don't have to justify things to me. Truthfully, I don't know how you put up with the constant attention and having your privacy invaded all of the time. It's no wonder you're close to a breakdown."

Jerricha sighed in agreement. Five nights ago, she'd collapsed while taking a break halfway through her St. Louis show and she'd barely been able to go back out on stage and finish, albeit, sitting on a hastily procured stool. She'd been on tour for the last ten months, and in between concerts and traveling around the world, she'd also found time to record a new album of Christmas songs that would be released on December twenty-first. Nine days from now.

Ben had wanted to add a whirlwind promotional Christmas tour to her already full schedule, but she'd put her foot down and refused. Kansas City had been her last scheduled performance on this tour, and she'd already announced she would take a sabbatical for the entire next year.

Ben had been furious with that decision, sure that she would become a has-been if she didn't keep producing new songs for her adoring and fickle fans. Jerricha didn't agree and she was willing to take that risk. She was tired, mentally, emotionally, and physically. Taking a year off had been her choice and since she could very well afford to do so, she wasn't seeking anyone's advice. She just wanted to be left alone and have time to find herself once again.

As for the band, well, they were all fine with having some time to party wherever the wind took them, and she knew that several of them were headed across the pond to hang out around Europe for a while. Part of her hoped they would all find other things to do during the next twelve months. If that happened, Ben would have no choice but to give her a shot at a solo career.

As far as the media was concerned, she was supposed to be flying to Tahiti to meet up with Bryce Lansing, a solo male pop singer who had shown an interest in her at a celebrity fundraiser she'd attended six months earlier. Since he was represented by the same record label, they'd been thrown together and rumors had been leaked that she and Bryce were having a secret relationship and would be making it public right after the first of the year.

The record label had been trying to boost Bryce's popularity and connecting him to Jerricha had been just the thing. His latest album had risen sharply in the polls, reaching the Top 10 within just a few weeks of his name being tied to hers. It hadn't really done a thing for Jerricha's career. Her fan base was one she'd been building since she'd first broken onto the music scene at nineteen.

The record label wanted to continue the façade, even hinting that they'd love to see a fake engagement sometime during January. Jerricha was adamantly against that idea, but Ben hadn't listened to her protests. She'd decided to take matters into her own hands.

She'd advanced her holiday plans a few weeks, and she wouldn't apologize for that to anyone. Warm Springs was her refuge and she was going to hibernate here for the winter, reconnect with her family and friends, and hopefully find the motivation to pick her life back up once again when the year was up. In a week or so, she'd send a message to one of the social media sites that usually made her life so miserable. She'd tell them of her terrible breakup with Bryce and then disappear for the next year. By the time she reappeared, her supposed breakup with Bryce would be old news and she could get back to her normal life.

Or not. She'd had fame and fortune and it wasn't all it was purported to be. She could easily go the rest of her life without signing another autograph or smiling for the camera alongside another celebrity looking to boost their popularity by being seen with her. In short, she was tired of being used.

As the small town came into view half an hour later, Jerricha felt a peace settle over her soul she'd not been able to find anywhere else in the world. "Welcome to Warm Springs."

She slowed the truck at the top of the small hill, bringing the vehicle to a stop on the snow-covered road, so that she could take in the familiar sight of mountains surrounding the small community. Snow covered the rooftops and lights already burned brightly in most of the homes, even though there were still several hours before the sun would disappear behind the mountains. Smoke rose in wisps from fireplaces and Jerricha couldn't stop the feeling of peace that settled over her soul. *Home. This is home.*

"It's like something out of a magazine," Cass whispered, the sight before them awe-inspiring to a city girl like her.

Jerricha nodded and then told her, "This place is sacred to me. No one knows about it except Ben and now you."

"The band members haven't been here before?"

Jerricha frowned and shook her head sharply. "No. I can't stand to be around those guys when we're not on stage. There was a time when we could laugh and joke with one another, but lately, they seem to be more into drugs and alcohol and women. I don't want any part of that lifestyle. Besides, can you imagine them in a place like this? No adoring groupies clamoring for their autograph or a quick tour of the bus. No photographers shoving cameras in their faces anytime they went out in public. They would be bored out of their minds within an hour, and they'd never appreciate the town for the gem it is."

"I've noticed there seems to be more and more partying happening. Is that why you stopped spending the night on the tour bus and started getting hotel rooms?"

Jerricha nodded. "Exactly. I explained it all to Ben and told him about my concerns. He assured me it's just a phase the guys are going through. Once they get used to how popular we are, they'll settle down and things will be back to normal."

"You don't believe him," Cass stated.

"No, I don't. I think Ben's assuming the guys will wake up one morning and realize how they're screwing up their lives, but they won't. They enjoy all the negative attention. I'm the one who's holding them back from even greater fame and fortune because I'm being the goody two shoes. They're afraid I'm going to try to go out on my own. My contract is up at the end of December and I haven't signed the renewal yet. I'm not sure I want to. I've kind of thought about going out on my own and doing my own thing for a while. No more tours. I can write and record…"

"That's not the worst idea I've ever heard. I mean, you write most of the songs now and sing them. You could become a solo act rather easy."

"Ben says the record label doesn't want a solo act. He doesn't, either. He wants to fill the stage with lights and videos, guitar licks, drum solos… the entire band experience."

Cass shook her head and made a sound of disapproval. "What do you want? I mean, without your voice, there is no *Jericho*. So, from where I sit, you hold all the cards."

Jerricha started up the truck again and headed down into the town. She couldn't stop thinking about Cass's question. *What do I want? What will make me truly happy?*

She'd kept herself from going down that mind path in the past, but now she had a little over two weeks in which to explore her feelings. Two weeks to take stock of her dreams and aspirations and measure them against the life she was currently living. Two weeks to measure them against the life she wanted to live. Two weeks to find the answer to Cass's question and set a course for her future happiness.

CATHEDRAL HILLS SERIES
    Book 1: JENNA AND TREY
    Book 2: MICHELLE AND TYLER
    Book 3: BROOKE AND PETER

IF YOU ENJOY MY BOOK(s), kindly help me by posting and sharing review(s) about my work – thank you!

Thank You

Dear Reader,

Thank you for choosing to read my books out of the thousands that merit reading. I recognize that reading takes time and quietness, so I am grateful that you have designed your lives to allow for this enriching endeavor, whatever the book's title and subject.

Now more than ever before, reader reviews and social media play vital roles in helping individuals make their reading choices. If any of my books have moved you, inspired you, or educated you, please share your reactions with others by posting a review as well as via email, Facebook, Twitter, Goodreads,—or even old-fashioned face-to-face conversation! And when you receive my announcement of my new book, please pass it along. Thank you.

For updates about New Releases, as well as exclusive promotions, visit my website and sign up for the VIP mailing list: www.morrisfenrisbooks.com[1]

I invite you to visit my Facebook page often facebook.com/AuthorMorrisFenris[2] where I post not only my news, but announcements of other authors' work.

For my portfolio of books on your favorite platform, please search for and visit my Author Page by typing **Morris Fenris** in the search bar of the relevant website.

You can also contact me by email: authormorrisfenris@gmail.com

With profound gratitude, and with hope for your continued reading pleasure,

Morris Fenris

Self-Published Author

---

1. http://www.morrisfenrisbooks.com
2. https://www.facebook.com/AuthorMorrisFenris/

Did you love *Brooke and Peter*? Then you should read *Sara in Montana*[3] by Morris Fenris!

What happens when a California girl in the middle of a crisis meets a Montana guy?

Sara wished for a husband for Christmas this year and then married her boss. Now she is running for her life from him, with a warrant out for her arrest, and really needs a miracle to save her. To top off her week, she finds herself in the middle of a Montana snowstorm and sicker than she's ever been.

Trent quit the FBI to return home and became a sheriff. As the most eligible bachelor in Castle Peaks, he's had his share of women chase him but has been disinterested; until now. He has a sworn duty to protect the town's citizens and assist other agencies in doing the same. When faced with a suspect in a criminal case, will he make the arrest or lead with his heart?

---

3. https://books2read.com/u/mYGzgw

4. https://books2read.com/u/mYGzgw

Join Sara Brownell as she runs for her life, straight into the waiting arms of local sheriff Trent Harding. Throw in a life-size nativity and plenty of snow, and watch the magic of Christmas come to life.

See how Sara forever changes the lives of Trent, as well as those around him.

Read more at https://www.facebook.com/AuthorMorrisFenris/.

About the Author

With a lifelong love of reading and writing, Morris Fenris loves to let his imagination paint pictures in a wide variety of genres. His current book list includes everything from Christian romance, to an action-packed Western romance series, to inspirational and Christmas holiday romance.

His novels are filled with emotion, and while there is both heartbreak and humor, the stories are always uplifting.

Read more at https://www.facebook.com/AuthorMorrisFenris/.

Made in the USA
Columbia, SC
18 June 2022